WHERE PEOPLE GO
WHEN THEY DIE IN WAR

WHAT READERS ARE DISCOVERING

The O Coalition Series is a sweeping spiritual fiction saga — part mystical encounter, part psychological healing, part Christ-centered awakening. Each novel follows an ordinary person who is unexpectedly drawn into a divine conversation that restores their true nature, reveals their spiritual gifts, and calls them into a life of purpose and love.

These stories blend the contemplative clarity of **Paulo Coelho (The Alchemist)**, the metaphysical adventure of **James Redfield (The Celestine Prophecy)**, and the soul-intimacy of **Richard Bach (JLS and Illusions)**, while grounding everything in authentic encounters with Christ, practical tools for emotional transformation, and real pathways to inner healing.

Through modern parables, visionary experiences, and dramatic real-world stakes, the series guides readers from brokenness to wholeness — revealing a path where spiritual gifts activate, old wounds dissolve, and God becomes intimately, undeniably real.

Readers learn alongside the characters — not just observing miracles, but experiencing shifts in their own hearts as they read.

More than novels, these books are **spiritual invitations**:

- to awaken to God's voice,
- to reconcile the self within,
- to release the wounds that distort,

• and to remember the divine identity already planted in every soul.

The O Coalition Series is for seekers who want **a story they can feel**, a story that transforms, a story that calls them — gently but unmistakably — into deeper union with God. Discover the full collection at theocoalition.com.

PRAISE FOR THE O COALITION BOOKS

BOOK ONE: THE LOWLY PROPHET

*"Heartfelt and thought-provoking… a blend of mystical experiences and relatable human struggles makes it an excellent choice **for readers interested in spirituality, mental health, or personal growth.**"*

— Literary Titan on Book One

BOOK TWO: THE VEIL BREAKER

*"The Veil Breaker is a surreal and emotionally raw journey through mental collapse and spiritual rebirth… I'd recommend it to seekers, to survivors of trauma, to anyone who's had a brush with mental illness or spiritual transformation and wants **a book that gets it.** Not in a clinical way, but in a gut-punch, soul-lifting, what-the-hell-just-happened kind of way."*

— Literary Titan on Book Two

BOOK THREE: WHERE PEOPLE GO WHEN THEY DIE IN WAR

*"I'm someone who has carried a great deal of loss and trauma. While reading this book, I realized it was speaking to me on a level deeper than understanding — it **reached right into my heart and soul.** Thomas's experiences resonated with my own in ways I didn't*

*expect, and I **felt seen, comforted, and gently transformed as the story unfolded.** This book doesn't just tell a story; it opens a door. Anyone who has ever suffered will find hope, healing, and a powerful reminder that God meets us right where we are."*

— Dr. James Chitwood, President, C-Suite for Christ Chicago

*"Mark Hattas has crafted something rare: a novel that operates as both **compelling narrative** and **practical spiritual roadmap**. Through Thomas's journey as a wartime healer, the book reveals a clear methodology for accessing God's voice and unlocking extraordinary gifts. The wartime setting serves as powerful metaphor: the real war is internal, between who we're trained to be and who **God created us to be**. The tools are real—releasing control, forgiving perceptions, seeking God internally—and immediately applicable. **Highly recommended** for seekers ready to move beyond theory into **lived experience of divine union**."*

— Stefan Junaeus, Founder, Thought Leaders Press

"Can humanity move from the battlefield, come forward to the field of God, and forego rising against one another? **This book catches you off guard, allowing you to pause and exhale**, individually or collectively, and rest assured of the answer."

— Dawn Kristy, JD - Founder, The Cyber Dawn ® Collective

WHERE PEOPLE GO WHEN THEY DIE IN WAR

MARK HATTAS

The. Coalition
POWERED BY Thought Leaders

DISCLAIMER:

This book is a work of fiction and is intended for educational and entertainment purposes only. The reader assumes full responsibility for any actions taken based on the content of this book. Nothing in this book is intended as a substitute for professional medical advice, diagnosis, or treatment.

To those seeking common ground in alignment with God's love. To those seeking peace where strife exists. To those open to seeing God at work in all things. This book is for you.

BEFORE YOU BEGIN
ENHANCE YOUR JOURNEY

Reading this book is an incredible journey on its own. However, like all The O Coalition stories, we offer an invitation to go beyond the book.

Why? The tools used by the characters are available to practice in your own life. So, you can heal inner turmoil as you explore the adventures in the book. Many have reported transformations as they read. However, as I know from personal experience, those can be temporary if not backed up with tools and discipline.

Whether you ever take any of our programs, know that tools and resources exist to support your well-being, and I pray you find your path to restored health and a restored **soul.**

What's Next? Explore the book's companion course and The O Coalition community (QR code).

If it's for you, I'll see you there.

ORIENTATION

What you are about to read is more than a story. It is a spiritual map integrated into fiction — a journey of awakening, reconciliation, and remembering who we truly are in God. Every character, every conflict, and every moment of healing mirrors our own inner world: the parts of us that suffer, the parts that rise, and the parts quietly waiting for God's touch.

Though set in a world torn by war, this book is ultimately about the war within — the division between the self we were trained to be and the self God created. As Thomas travels through visions, teachings, and encounters with Christ, you may find your own hidden places illuminated. His healing is not meant to be admired; it is meant to awaken your own. And as that awakening unfolds, your spiritual gifts — the ones God placed in you from the beginning — may stir, unlock, and begin to reveal themselves.

This story will not simply be read; it will be felt. You may notice warmth rising in your chest, a softening behind the eyes, or an old ache loosening as you travel with Thomas. These are not accidents. God meets us in sensation, in breath, in the quiet spaces beneath thought. As you move through these chapters, let your soul lean forward. Something in you already remembers the way home.

This book was written for readers hungry for truth, weary of division, and ready for a deeper relationship with God. The miracles, teachings, and experiences woven through these pages are inspired by countless real encounters — my own and those of people I've accompanied in their spiritual journeys. Christ is alive and moving today, and the same Presence guiding Thomas is available to you.

If you let it, this story will work on you. It will soften old judgments, reveal hidden wounds, and invite the healing that comes when we surrender to God's love. And as healing comes, expect your gifts — intuition, discernment, vision, compassion, creativity, spiritual sensitivity — to rise toward their fullness. Read slowly. Listen inwardly. Let the Spirit teach you in the space between the sentences.

Let's go. You are about to walk deeper into your faith journey — into the lived experience of becoming another Christ in the world, with the gifts God designed uniquely for you.

A War on Humanity is Upon Us and
There is an Answer for Peace

CHAPTER 1
SHATTERING SILENCE

My mind was at peace, yet my heart shattered.

With a jolt, I was thrown to the ground. Dust filled my lungs on impact. Pressing my elbow into the dirt, I slowly rose to one knee. The barren earth lay waste in every direction—my view partially blocked by a militarized beast towering over my helpless body. A loud, forceful sound-wave struck my ears, slamming me flat again. Covering my bloodied ears, I squinted at an oncoming dust cloud racing behind a colorful, visible sound tsunami. The waves looked like heat shimmering above a hot road.

These acoustic weapons, though non-lethal, were more painful than I had realized. It was my first time on the receiving end. My government's weapons were being used on me, violently shaking the atmosphere, rattling my soul.

As the sound echoed through my skull and numbed my senses, I mentally retreated to the recesses of my psyche, fading in and out of consciousness. The world muted as my thoughts thrust forward:

We are all weapons of my destruction.

I did this.

I made it happen.

I found God and trespassed on that sacred domain of cause and effect.

Years ago a doctor had told me I was insane. I tried his medications and crumbled into a pit of horror. My sense of self always came into view in heaven. I knew that heavenly state was where I would actually heal. But how could I heal with five times the recommended medicines restraining my system—a daily barrage of chemical aerial bombs detonating inside me?

Of course I needed to heal on all sides—inside, outside, on-side, down-side, up-side—every side. Not just my body, but my interior life; my soul needed healing. This is crazy, but heaven is there. It is here. I found it.

I felt free until I succumbed to the doc's drugs, trapped in a loop of a medically induced psychedelic morass. I pray for freedom. Someone must remind humanity of its true nature. We must be freed from the lies caging us in our own minds. The keys to freedom are in hand. They must be shared.

I pray that I live and serve this mission. Freedom! Freedom! God, may my soul remember you. I lay myself on the altar of our Lord.

God awaits our acceptance of this invitation. I pray that all who are lost, dangerous, insane, broken, or merely disinterested in life let Christ in—for that is God's antidote to madness, to brokenness, to all of it—and it's free.

My mental respite was interrupted by the brief return of ringing in my ears and a pounding in my head before it withdrew once again. I am where I am because I ignored God. I lost my way. I must return and teach what I'm learning.

People... they worry about getting to Heaven. The doorway has been opened. They need only open their eyes to see it. They must drop all judgments and forgive sins. The path is holy. It is accessible. It is here.

I recall Hercules, who failed to navigate his inner world—consequently destroying his outer world. His twelve labors were atonement. His inner journey of self-discovery, redemption, and spiritual transformation can be our journey. But instead of waiting for it, I propose we prioritize the inside before the outside defeats us.

I'm ready.

A breath rushed in as my eyes opened to Pablo's familiar boots, marked by a Hello Kitty skull and crossbones sticker. A gun most certainly was pointed at my head. My bloody hands wiped at my ears, trying to shake through the disturbing confusion. The deafening ringing subsided, and distant shouting of military commands came into focus. Time had slowed considerably. I reconsidered all that I knew. All my constructs were shaken, and new truths, realities, and wisdom penetrated. I contemplated whether the acoustic weapons were accidentally opening the heavens, bringing answers for our war-torn world.

Despite being attacked, I suddenly felt a great love for my persecutors. a love that melted anger and rage. A calming breath loosened the pressure in my head, as if peace itself had entered with the inhale.

I looked up to see Pablo's face. Goggles covered his eyes. A helmet protected his ears and head. But I knew it was him.

CHAPTER 2
MY FRIEND PABLO

D espite his menacing stare and current disposition, Pablo had been a friend many years earlier. We grew up together.

While some kids played farmer or warrior or house, Pablo and I pretended I was a saint and he was a demon. He would climb onto my bedpost and whisper ugly messages of torment as I prayed for his soul. I pretended not to care about his insults. After all, it was just a game. But they felt real. I never thought he was role-playing; I thought he was telling me who he really was.

Games were one thing, but as he stood over me with a gun in my face, this was no game. He was tormenting me with real ill intent.

As he holstered his gun, I noticed the dusty whip attached to a weathered belt—his favorite weapon used against anyone who crossed his boss. He seemed all too happy to find me and reached for my hand.

"Cut the crap, Pablo. You just knocked me to the ground.

Why would you lift me up?" I asked, wiping the blood on my shirt. I was ragged, filthy. "How did we get here, my friend? Who are you beneath this facade? Your betrayal of self now carries over to me. Underneath your evil is good." I did everything I could to remain centered, calm.

He looked at me with coldness, empty eyes, a calloused face. It wasn't my friend I saw there. His soul was hidden, guarded by distortion—held captive by a crooked regime, those behind the madness. I remember first meeting one of their leaders when I was just sixteen. He showed up at my home with a few others, full of smiles and energy. Very slick. I had a reputation as a healer by that point—a gift quite remarkable even in the early days. He asked if I would pray to help their friend heal and pointed to a young man lying in the back of a jeep. It was my first job for the regime.

Their friend healed, praise be our Beloved. Because of that, word spread, and I traveled the world speaking, teaching, and healing. I went wherever I was needed. Once the war broke out, the regime wanted me home. Reluctant, I was compelled to return. People were dying, and I could help.

My attention turned back to Pablo. I felt sadness. While I had experienced great adventures meeting leaders around the world, he had stayed home working odd jobs until Nancy, a recruiter for the regime, noticed him loading hay bales on a tractor bed at her neighbor's farm. They never dated, but I imagine her pretty smile and buff physique were more interesting to Pablo than the regime's objectives. They hid it well, but under the facades and propaganda their actions were against the people. Pablo wasn't the only one duped. Sadness weighed heavily as I contemplated the changes in my friends and our world.

Pablo had been one of my best friends until he became a soldier. He bought into their narratives, blinded to what was obvious to anyone willing to see. Perhaps losing Pablo to them was to be expected. Perhaps our childhood game of angels and demons foreshadowed our futures. My memory of his demon presence stood tall in my mind, my heart, and my soul; the pain remained unresolved as he stood over me on that barren land.

I worked for the regime too, but for very different reasons. I had grown tired and sick of the circumstances, so I left. When the regime first sought me out, I believed I was serving God. They called me "Priest," though I was little more than a medic of the soul. I prayed over the wounded, laid hands, and spoke light into darkness. I told myself every healed soldier was one less soul lost to despair. But when I saw those same men sent back to the battlefield, I realized I was not healing the world—I was helping it destroy itself. That's when I left, not in rebellion, but in repentance.

My conscience would not let me rest. I wandered for months seeking redemption until God gave me one name—Pablo. I thought returning for him might redeem us both.

What I hoped to find in villages outside ours—hope to restore me to a healthy state and ultimately end the war—was nowhere to be found. So I returned and sought out Pablo, not to be attacked but to convince him to come with me. He was my only hope. The world felt empty; I felt alone. Demon or not, I thought I could sway him. I was wrong.

"I've got him," I heard Pablo report through his walkie-talkie.

"Bring him to me. Good job," came the reply.

With hands cuffed and earmuffs to protect my ears, we marched. Well, he marched. I shuffled, stumbled, and even tripped occasionally.

While walking, I looked over at him, recalling us as kids. A smile struck across my face despite his expressionless look, his head pivoting on alert for threats. We played in my backyard often: tag, ghost in the graveyard, angels and demons. We had a lot of fun. My sister used to play, filling various roles, acting as if she could rule the world. He liked her despite being five years her senior.

Why anyone would like my sister at that age—she was around seven—made no sense. I caught him stealing glances at her as I would at girls my age. I think she liked the attention, but it seemed weird to me. He couldn't keep his eyes off her. He wouldn't just look at her like you might a cute kid; he laser-focused like an eagle on prey. Feeling uncomfortable, I called him out. He denied it and struck. Reacting, I said some awful things, including that he must have an abusive home to be that cruel. Instantly his right hook landed before I knew he had swung. Years later I learned I had been right about the abusive home.

Victims are funny. I could have blamed myself, but I never understood what he saw in my sister. Was she a target? Salvation? A distraction? He was a wild rabbit running scared, quenching a thirst for normalcy, safety, surety—sacrifice possibly. I didn't know. I just knew from that day forward he couldn't be around my sister.

It was the last playdate we had. Seventh grade. I hated seventh grade. I hated him. I cried every day for a week. That was the moment our friendship died.

Years later, when the regime rose and began recruiting, I heard Pablo had joined them. By then we were long estranged—the distance between us no longer just miles but years of silence. I told myself our break was old history, yet when I saw him again—armored, armed, hollow-eyed—it felt like losing him all over. The boy who once played demon had become one, and I prayed he could remember who he was before the darkness claimed him.

As we walked, I collapsed inside my mind—all those stories and tangled emotions folding in on themselves. I looked him over—war-torn, battle-fatigued, confused. Twisting, I grabbed his hand and felt a jolt of energy. He stopped, met my eyes.

"Pablo, I pray for your soul, that the Light of Christ be within you. Bless you, bless you, bless you."

He jerked his hand away. "Shut up, you fool. Move it."

We walked for what felt like miles beneath the blistering sun. The land was scorched, silent, stripped of mercy. As the horizon shimmered, a vast structure rose from the dust—a temple once devoted to prayer, now defiled into a military stronghold. The regime called it their compound, but to me it was a tomb.

The entire base had grown around the temple, as if the regime's power depended on desecrating what was once sacred. Barracks and command tents sprawled outward from its ancient walls—a web of machinery and control feeding off the heart of worship. What had been a sanctuary became the pulse of their empire. As we drew closer, I could feel the residue of holiness beneath the noise—the faint hum of prayers long silenced, waiting to rise again.

The outer walls of the temple were carved from white stone, now blackened by smoke. Guards patrolled the perimeter while drones circled like vultures. Beyond the gates, rows of tents and medical checkpoints waited—the army's wounded ushered inside for what they called my miracles.

I remembered the temple's design: ring upon ring of rooms and courtyards. The outer court overflowed with soldiers—some groaning, some already still. Conventional medics worked beside me there, but my presence meant something different. They believed if the Priest was there, God still fought on their side.

Pablo pushed me toward the Commander's tent, the sound of boots striking dirt echoing like a dirge. I had prayed this meeting might mark the end of my wandering—that I could bring one lost soul into alliance. Instead, it felt like the gates of my old prison swinging shut.

Commander Charles stood before us, gilded in arrogance—his uniform unwrinkled, his skin untouched by war, his eyes bright with the cruelty of conviction. He smiled the way serpents smile before striking.

"Ah, you've chosen to return, my good and faithful servant."

He twisted those sacred words into mockery.

"No," I said, my voice thin but steady. "I have not returned to serve you. I serve only God."

"Right, right," he sneered. "Then remember—it is your God who gave you these gifts. Use them. My soldiers need you." He motioned to Pablo. "Get him to the temple. The Priest will heal again. Praise be to God!"

I resisted, but my hands, once called forth to bless, were bound. In that instant I understood—I was not simply being taken captive by men, but by the unfinished part of my own soul that still feared its own power. God was not punishing me; He was purifying me.

Yet I still felt defeated. In my imagination, Pablo would have woken from his distortion and we would have canvassed the planet to find help. Instead, I was right back where I had begun just weeks earlier.

I climbed the narrow ladder to my old perch overlooking the chaos. The air was thick with iron and incense. I remembered when this space had once felt alive with prayer; now, every cry was a distortion of worship. I struggled for my sanity within the temple walls. Where was our sanity? Why? What was the point in killing men, women, and children? Whose madness were we carrying out anyway?

Before my escape and subsequent return, I'd been at that temple post for years, thinking my work would change the tide of our leaders. I had hoped they would change and see another way. Their path continued to bring our world deeper into dark-ness. I thought of going out into the world to find people who had power and could change the trajectory of the destruction. I prayed to Jesus for help and found an answer: go from the temple and seek assistance in the world.

Leaving everything behind, I left one night—excited to embark on this quest, angry that our leaders only wanted me to heal soldiers so they could be redeployed and fight once more. Our Commander was a tyrant, an animal. I wished him dead more than once. In fact, I wanted to kill him—and I could have. I just hadn't. Perhaps I was a coward. Perhaps I had been blinded by hate, a hate that surfaced in those temple years.

9

Unfortunately, I found more enemies outside the temple walls. I sought after the good guys and gals, but my emotions clouded my sight. It seemed none could be found. I came across camps, villages, and cities. Hundreds of miles I traveled, doing my best to stay clear of known battlefields.

One camp I neared looked promising. I saw fires and dozens of permanent tents that lined two makeshift roads meeting at a cross in the middle. Four guard posts stood at the end of each makeshift street. Oddly, the place appeared empty when I arrived. Walking toward the far end, near a cliff's edge, I heard a commotion—the sounds of wild animals and people hollering. Eight people had been stripped naked and were being marched to the cliff. I quickly ducked behind a large old tree and peered out, hoping I hadn't been spotted.

The captured men and women were read their rights and informed that rabid animals would be released upon them. Anyone who survived would be offered a position in the camp's army. These were the consequences for their crimes. The crimes were unstated. One couple locked eyes and reached for each other's hands. They were the first to take a leap of faith that the rocks below would be more forgiving than their captors. Five others followed. Three fought for their lives. One survived.

I was horrified, and upon nightfall I quickly moved east until finding a village two days later. I prayed its inhabitants would be clothed and hospitable. Observing from a distance, I could see only men in the village. They looked weak and despondent. A mass grave revealed their loved ones recently slaughtered. I felt disgusted, discouraged, hopeless. Traveling north, south, east, and west for weeks reinforced a humanity compromised, distorted, strange… destroyed.

A nomad lost amidst chaos, I camped by myself for three nights. As I stopped chasing some powerful, sane, loving person or group to help, I settled in with God. God reminded me to address my hate, my anger, my fear, and soon I was hearing God's voice clearly. "Thomas, it's time to go. You must return." I saw an image of Pablo in my mind and asked if I was to seek him out. "Yes," came the inner prompt from God's holy way.

At first I resisted. Pablo had chosen his path long ago, and I wanted to believe it was too late for him to change. But then God showed me the truth—that no soul is beyond return. Even the hardest hearts are only walls built from pain. The light of Christ waits behind every wall, patient, unhurried.

I understood then that going back for Pablo wasn't only about saving him; there was something to heal in me too. If I could see the divine in him, then perhaps the divine in me could be restored as well. Love had to go where hatred ruled.

My desperation to leave such a despicable world paused as God's prompt showed me a new path forward. I packed up and began my return home.

From a distance, I saw Pablo on patrol. Trusting God's prompt, I walked closer, thinking we could talk. I hoped he would remember our early friendship and previous love for each other. I hoped he would leave with me to go to the one place I hadn't dared to go alone—our enemies—to convince them to stop the war. I tried to convince him of my plan, that there was another way to establish peace.

He wouldn't even look me in the eyes, let alone listen. He was afraid. I tried to run, but his gun hit the back of my head. As I turned, he pistol-whipped me, shoved me to the ground, and called in my capture.

CHAPTER 3
MY FAVORITE
MEMORY FROM WAR

The temple perch gave me much time to pray and think. That, plus my daydreams muted the toxic energy of the people in control. I could no longer bear it, nor could I run again. My soul felt lost, confused. Though praying frequently, I sometimes questioned why. In the days following my capture, instead of praying for the soldiers' health, I asked for God's love to guide me through that one day.

Surrendering in this way, memories often surfaced with lessons to learn or revisit. One day, my favorite memory since the war started surfaced:

My hope had grown brittle. Each morning, I awoke to the same ache: to pray or not to pray? I still spoke God's name, but the words hung hollow in my chest. I wanted a sign—not of power, but of presence. Something to prove I hadn't imagined His nearness.

It happened at a hotel in one of the cities I had recently

visited. A young woman arrived with her five children like a shepherd with a living flock—one balanced on her hip, two dragging tired feet, the others helpful at her side. Her hands were full, and her exhaustion was holy to me. I offered to help. She shared that her husband was at war while I carried their bags to their room. Upon arriving, I asked if I could somehow repay her kindness.

"Why would you ask that?" she asked, confused. "You helped us!"

"No," I replied. "You helped me."

"How so?" she inquired further.

"I was considering leaving for good." I responded. With her children around, I kept it cryptic, but she could see in my eyes what I meant. "I prayed just before you arrived at the hotel that if our Beloved Creator truly desired for me to remain here, a woman would arrive with five children carrying luggage and needing assistance."

She looked at me perplexed, saying, "Well, it is a hotel. Isn't it likely that there could be a woman with children who would need some help?"

"Five children," I corrected her. "And yes, it is possible, so I asked if it's the woman you sent, Lord, have her pay me $500 found on the route to the hotel."

Her surprised expression leaked through her efforts to suppress it. "It is true that my son found $500 on route to this hotel. However, you have no idea whether I was going to give it to you or not."

"No, I don't," I replied. "Were you planning to give me that $500?"

"Yes, she was," her oldest son piped up.

"Oh, shush," she said to him. "Okay, you are correct. I did tell our children to give it to the first person who showed kindness to our family. So, thank you, dear sir. You are the first person in three days to show kindness to us." She reached into her purse, took out the $500, and handed it to me.

The memory dissolved like smoke, and I realized my knees were pressed against the same cold stone where I had been praying. The temple's medicinal air was heavy so I relit the thurible's coals to refresh the air and remind me of my holy place. As I sat on the temple perch, recalling that encounter, tears fell, just as they had when the event occurred. God's love had come and reminded me of who I absolutely, unequivocally am, a child of our Beloved. My life was to be lived.

After the encounter, I took that $500 to my sister's house. She was astonished, praising God for answering her need for money. I laughed, realizing my actions had answered her prayer, the woman at the hotel had answered mine, and some unknown traveler had answered hers. If there was ever an example that God lives within us, this was one for me, and I prayed, giving thanks for the eyes to see such a miracle.

Inspired by that beautiful memory, I rose on the perch and pressed both palms to the cool stone. Incense now mingled with the bite of iron; from below came the hush of stretchers and the soft clink of instruments. I prayed out loud—so loudly that everyone in the outer court could hear. Many bowed their heads or lifted their arms in praise of receiving a miracle:

"Our beloved has come today. Open your hearts and reach for the skies as this love opens in you what you most need. Let the skies of heaven come into you now, releasing all hurts, wounds, and pain. May the glories of God come into your life immediately upon request, going where that love is needed most, healing all divisions, restoring every holy part. Let these words fall like rain upon this very court, upon these cots, these weary brows, and trembling hands. Let heaven touch the earth here, now.

"Embrace this love now as you look to the one next to you. Reach and touch, letting the infinite power of God's holy universal healing power permeate the friend or foe beside you, healing all that they most need."

With that, I saw patients sitting up and rolling over to reach for their neighbor. Many doctors and nurses joined in the prayer, and it became clear that a special atmosphere had been created in the temple that day. All inspired by a memory that came through the depth of my despair. Still personally reeling from the pain Pablo had inflicted, I suddenly felt a loving embrace. A nurse had reached up and touched my foot. Her hand trembled, but the trembling passed into me as peace. I had spent years shielding myself from pain; now even another's touch could heal. I prayed, "God, I request you here now. I welcome you" I felt movement, energy shifts, and changes in my body-mind system—a reorientation throughout my whole physical, mental, and emotional structures. Love had returned. Love restored me. "God, you are truly here."

I sat back down, realizing in some strange way I had defied the evil in me by praying—my anger, hate, and hurt. I was so happy and thankful that I could no longer resist the active forces of God that compelled me to stand and pray as I had.

There was a time when I didn't trust God, and resistance to God's ways was effortless. I was a child then, viewing God outside of myself, humanizing God as an authority figure trying to control me. A lot has changed since those days. Defying God as I spiritually matured became difficult and eventually debilitating.

Imagine having a thought of making a meal and then fighting yourself. Why would you do that? You wouldn't. If you were clear. You would just make the meal. This is how I usually was with God. If I were called to pray, I prayed. We prayed. How prayers got answered was beyond me. But trusting God was important, and this holy memory helped me restore that.

CHAPTER 4
FLOWER IN THE DESERT

As people stirred below following the healing prayer, I closed my eyes to center on the temple perch. Another memory took center stage in my mind. I was ten years old when I finished my morning prayers. A mental image of a cat surfaced. I didn't know what the image was for, and used the opportunity to ask God for a cat. I imagined feeling love from this cat. Then I saw a mental image of a water well. It wasn't a well I was exactly familiar with, but looked similar to the one in our neighbor's backyard. They had a farmhouse down the road. I ignored the message, for I didn't know that divine *messages* were possible at that time. Days later, I heard a cat was found dead in our neighbors' well.

I felt horrible. I had denied clear communication from the heavens and was determined to listen from then on. Divine messages continued frequently, but the shame of ignoring that first one haunted my psyche for some time. I questioned why I ignored the image. Why didn't I have a reference for how God speaks? What was wrong with my parents, my teachers, and our pastor, who claimed to teach about God? How could I just let that cat die?

The shame over that cat lingered for years. I carried it like a curse—a reminder of my deafness to God. Then a friend invited me to a Navajo ceremony promising a holy restoration through medicine used to reveal hidden truths. I went not to chase visions, but to listen and heal pain. The medicine woman prepared the fire, her movements prayerful. I entered their circle in search of reconciliation. The cedar smoke curled into my chest; I let it. *Not my will, Lord—make me ready.*

As I took a seat, the shame still clung to me like burrs on wool. I prayed for a way to unclench what my mind hadn't released. The medicine woman explained the ritual, the songs, the circle, and the safeguards. I set my intentions aloud—*be free of the blame resting in my soul, see the truth, and hear God without distortion.* Only then, with consent and reverence, did I receive the medicine.

The air shimmered as the medicine took root in my body. A hum rose in my ears—part wind, part heartbeat. The fire seemed to breathe, expanding and contracting with me. Heat pressed on my skin. The spirit of God moved me to my feet.

Under its influence for the first time, I soon wandered off into the barren trails of the Reservation. Our medicine woman, having administered the concoction, allowed me to wander under her watchful eye. My vision softened; outlines melted into light. The desert breathed like a living thing. In that stillness, form and spirit exchanged places—everything spoke. From the brush emerged an antelope asking me for a "spot of tea." The world rearranged itself into vision-logic; creatures took on voices, and symbols spoke plainly. I didn't have any tea and so inquired why the antelope would like tea.

"You wandered the desert, came to me, and I have a desire to speak. I like to have tea when I have company," the antelope said

"I see. What is it that you would like to speak about?" I asked.

"I think you know what I want to speak about. I want to call your mother."

Since my mother had passed four years prior, it was a curious conversation. "Okay," I said. "Call my mother."

The antelope rolled over, and a phone opened up inside its belly. I reached, and upon touching the phone, my mother spoke to me.

"I am here, son. I have come to answer a question you must hear. Speak no more. And now we begin…" Her words didn't just enter my ears; they entered my blood. Every syllable quivered through me like a tuning fork struck by heaven.

She continued. "Once upon a time, there was a boy who was very, very brave. One day, a man the boy perceived as wise, with a long, hairy beard, came to him and told him he was a bad person. This harsh judgment planted a seed of disease in the boy's mind, a seed that sprouted torment and all types of horrible images in the garden of deception.

"Today, this boy lives inside a man. He cries himself to sleep. He wishes for death, but there's an answer that requires mystical energies to come to the boy. He will become a great saint, someone whom people look to for guidance, support, and health restoration. You are that boy, son. You are that person. Trust in God, and you will have all you need to do it. Release trying to control. Allow for God. If you are to become that man, you must go and save yourself from the torment you created."

A heat rose in me — not from the desert fire, but from the boy I'd buried. My fists clenched. "That I created?" I spat. "How can you even say that? You, who failed to teach me the ease through which I could hear God's voice? You, who shamed my siblings when they were wrong? You, who silenced the divine rising in me? Wasn't it you who opened me to years of torment?" My breath came sharp, my body trembling. The desert blurred. Rage spoke the language of my abandoned youth. The boy wanted a mother; the man wanted a verdict.

"Yes, I did those things," she admitted.

"Then what would you have me do? Why is it that you lied to me?"

"No, I did not lie. I didn't believe."

"Believe? Believe?! What do you mean?" My anger and vitriol surged, overflowing and projecting like darts aimed through the phone, at her heart, her throat, her head—anywhere I could penetrate the evil I heard before me. Die, I thought in my heart of hearts. Die. I just wanted to destroy this person who spoke to me, my mother.

She interrupted my turmoil. "I was wrong, son. I shared all I could. You know yourself more than I ever could. You share life with the world. I cowered, fearing repercussions from it. Now I see. I feared the judgment of our neighbors, the church and God. Worldly approval meant too much to me."

The words pierced me. My throat tightened. For years I had begged to hear her say those two words: *I was wrong.*

She continued, "Thomas, you have come to share wisdom to help people restore life. You were created in the image of God, to live as one, yet you hold to this concept that I and others deceived you. We did not deceive you. You did. We cared. We brought you into this world. We taught you what we had to teach. It's your life now. You can change things today. Or, you can limit your potential by holding on to me as evil in your mind. That hurts you, not me. You created that image of me. Let go of it—all of it. Let Christ show you what is true."

The desert wind stilled. I felt the heat lift from my chest, and her voice took on form. She stood on the trail — ragged clothes, hair tangled, eyes hollow. My body trembled as the earth seemed to tremble with me. Dust coiled around her like a veil torn from heaven's fabric.

"If you believe that your mother is what you see before you," she said, "you have deceived yourself, son. Let me go. Let me leave, and you will see the true nature of your mother."

"How do you suppose I do that? How do you suppose I just release something that's true?"

"Only true in the image you made, son. Let the image go, and truth will remain. Collapse the image of who you see before you by praying."

I fell to my knees as she gave me the prayer. The words came from the depth of my soul. "In the name of God, Creator of me, I command truth, light, healing, purity, to come into this image..." My voice shook. Tears hit the sand like rain. "...and allow it to shift gently or violently, whatever is in my highest and best interest. I release now what I've created about Mom. Restore me to see who she is truly."

As I spoke the words my eyes pressed closed. A wind filled my lungs. The little boy in me cried out for love. Memories, beliefs, and identifications raced through my mind. *God, come here now, come here,* I thought.

I was no longer in control, unable to open my eyes or move. An image of God appeared in my mind as clear as if my eyes were open—a light so bright that I couldn't look directly into it without bending forward touching my forehead to the ground. My cells radiated with purpose, transforming my perception of Mom.

The air cracked. My breath moved and my eyes popped open. The lie dissolved before my eyes, and Mom knelt beside me, embracing me, love radiating from her. She was radiant, confident, free. The false mother dissolved, and the true one — the holy one — stood before me. No more pain. Only love. It was wonderful!

"Now go forth and do what you came to do," she said, her hands warm upon my face. "Let the freedom you've found carry God's words through you to the world. Continue disorienting the parts you hold falsely as *gospel* within you. The process you just completed with me—apply it to your father and to all in your life." She touched my throat, and light spread through me — soft at first, then blazing. A judgment-induced curse of reluctance broken. Voice restored to witness.

My eyes opened; my heart thumped. She was gone, and in her place was a beautiful flower, freshly emerging from the death grip of a crusted Earth. I picked the flower up, placed it behind my right ear, and trekked back to where I had started. Somewhere a hawk cried, clean and bright. I felt lighter, filled with joy.

"I see you found some life in our desert land." The medicine woman looked a lot like my mom, and she knew I had been healed. Radiating kindness, she took me back into a hut-like structure called a Hogan. The others who had participated in the ceremony had awaited my return, and I took a seat by the fire.

The medicine woman broke the silence, encouraging me to share with the group. "You have returned from the wilderness, and we now welcome you and invite you to reveal what you have discovered."

"I found my mom. I suppose I had clothed her with false images. Some might call it distortion, evil, or hate. Every book has its way of conveying how distortions, curses, and other things happen. We do it to ourselves, and it's through our willingness they are freed. My mom is not what I thought she was, but is a reflection of the holiest of holies, doing in this world what she was here for. She gave me life. She taught me in the ways, and I know I'm free to live. I'm free, and that is my mind saying that. My mind says something magical and mystical occurred out in that desert, and now something pure, innocent, and easy has replaced what was hard, ugly, and distorted. I'm thankful and so happy!"

"Where did you get the flower?" a young girl sitting on her mother's lap asked me.

"My mother gave it to me. A gift she promised when I was a boy. I'd gone to her when I was sad and asked, 'Mom, why is it that you are so mean to me? What is it that I'm here for?' She said there would come a time upon this Earth when I would know, and at that time, the universe would reveal to me a flower—a common flower reflecting the simplicity of the brilliance of God. Today, in the desert, she gave it to me. Thank you, Mom!"

When the desert experience revealed my mom as innocent, I felt ashamed that I hadn't known the truth. I questioned all of my beliefs.

What else is untrue? Where am I deceiving myself? Where am I and what is life for? Christ in me, tell me why I am here.

Christ responded, "Everyone is to come home. I'm where you are, and always am where you are. I came for you and love you. You are on the right path.

My inner turmoil continued, despite feeling comforted that I was on the right path. For, it didn't change the path I was on. I cried out, *"But God, why? Why not let everyone be healed, whole, integrated? Is it too big for you? Is it more than you can co-create with humans? Is it hard? What is it that you have us doing here? Who is it that you think I am?"*

"I think you are a Christ," God replied.

"What do you mean?" I asked.

"You are the bread of life, the one who knows himself as he is. You are that which you are. All of yourself is given to God. It is this remembrance that everyone is invited into. You are whole, Thomas, and I am happy with you. I accept you. I love all of you."

"You mean I, a person of so many faults, is loved wholly by you? And you call me a Christ?"

"Yes. I created you in my image. You are my child, my son. All can discover this, as you have; reuniting with me as you learn who you are. Then we rejoice together in the resurrection of life and joy of reconciliation. One of you may stray so that others choose to stay. The gift of the "strays" is the strengthening of my bond with humanity as all are called *home*. It fosters conviction for your mission. You will know yourself, you know me, and our wills unite as one.

"Why now? Why me?" I asked.

"For I am I am, and you thought I would never come. You perceived us as separate. You wanted to go about your day, having a grand old time, defying your insights; defying all that you know. You did what you needed to do to give yourself an expression of life. I am all, and you are part of me. We are one. Can you see me?"

"Yes, I see you and know that I falsely clothed you, as I had my mother. Forgive me. I release clothing of you, God, with false images. Make me whole always. I surrender."

This led to an inner dialogue unwinding distortions I had clothed God with. My anger fell, revealing insecurities and worries. Soon, those transformed as roots of faith took hold in my heart. I felt God *trim the dead limbs* from my *trunk*. An insight surfaced about an unconscious, suppressed desire to *kill God*, but actually I only wanted the false image I had created of God to dissolve—to be reunited with the one true God. Eager to have that false image *die*, I asked God, "How do I do this?"

"You may go and act as you will, but know this—the effects of every action will come swiftly. When you see how quickly straying from love disturbs your peace, you'll move just as quickly to return to it. In time, you'll learn to wander less and less, until your heart chooses no sin at all. Along that way, you will come to know Me, and I will make My home in you completely."

"I want this, but I've collected so much evidence against you, and the people who've hurt me. Lord, I no longer wish to carry this. What do I do with it?"

"You lay it down by saying, 'Holy Father, I've been wrong. I've made mistakes. Please remove these errors from my soul. Please forgive me and purify in the name of the Father and of the Son and of the Holy Spirit. Amen.'"

I said the prayer, and immediately God was teaching me again. I was home and felt a hero's energy—peace. It was like the end of the original Star Wars, when the heroes were center screen, celebrated with accolades. That is how I felt hearing God's wisdom guide me. It changed my heart. Prior to that, I tried caring, but after that desert healing, I genuinely cared.

I saw then that my arrogance had never been defiance against God—it was disbelief that His mercy could reach me. Pride had been a mask for fear. When that fear dissolved, I could finally love freely.

Coming out of my prayer, I sensed people were looking at me. I opened my eyes to see people gathered below, saying, "You healed me." "You saved my life!" "You are a hero." "You are God's true disciple."

This was common, but incorrect. I did not do what they are projecting onto me. Like I created false images in my past, they were at risk of doing the same with me.

I corrected them, calling down. "Please gather here now. I have a message you must hear about why you were healed." People picked up their mats, walked, and gathered together below me. There were a few who sat toward the front, exclaiming the glories of God or of me. A few hung near the back, waiting to hear what I might say. Most of the crowd huddled together in the middle, looking up, awaiting the message.

What they didn't understand was that my words were God's words. Most think that I came up with them. They believe I am doing the healing. When we are transformed in Christ, the person we once were is no more. The new person is why I do what I do. It is this new Christ that is born, replacing the old self. And as a Christ, one knows and has memory of the old self. A Christ remembers, but knows of himself as a human being; everything of his new self is only of God. Thus, the lips that spoke the prayer opening their faith to healing were no longer the lips of my old self, but lips speaking God's words. I recognize and witness God's words—words not only for them, but equally for me..

God spoke through me once again. "Ladies and gentlemen, I have three messages for you today. First, no man or woman can ever heal any idea in their mind until they surrender the idea in their mind. Second, everyone here heals because of their faith. There are reasons your mind gives you as it tries to make sense of things. Let your mind relax, and release your conclusions.

"Imagine seeing an airplane for the first time! You would have looked to the skies and wondered, 'What a marvel. What a mystery! What magical creature may have been flying such a device?' Of course, you all know what an airplane is, and you know how it works. You know about airplanes. Regarding healing, you can look at this dynamic as unusual, a mystery. Or, you can look upon this and recognize that all you experienced here is a concept, like that first airplane, that has yet to propagate through consciousness such that you know it as easily as you know other things.

"If you can accept that there's energy you have available to heal, then you can say, 'I allow for my system to be fully healthy, and all that might be in the way of health I choose to change. In the name of the Creator of all things, I invite holy ideas to enter my mind to bring about actions I can take in support. I allow this, and I accept all that comes in my system to heal in the name of the Father, the Son, and the Holy Spirit. Amen.'

"Once you do this, you proceed to recognizing that Christ is available to each and every one of you. You can choose to die from where you have been, and come forward into new life, the *field* of God where God gives you rest. If you would like to enter into a whole relationship with God, simply make a conscious choice. In that relationship you will know the one true God, the Alpha and the Omega, the I am I am."

Men and women cried out. They wanted it. The hunger was building. Change was coming.

CHAPTER 5
MY SILLY FRIEND, MARY

Days had blurred together inside the temple; prayer was my only clock. Alone once again on my perch, I prayed quietly. Naturally, the people in the temple knew me only as I was, a spiritual master teacher and healer. They didn't see the depths of the creation process—the foundation being poured, the walls built, plumbing and electrical installed—a *house* built by my Father in Heaven for this time so many years later. One formative memory surfaced among many —one that had shaped me over years. The temple air was still. Beneath the silence, I felt the pulse of God like a second heartbeat. Then the boy I once was stirred within me.

Imagine a ten-year-old boy, me, sitting in my bedroom alone —my short brown hair recently cut for a wedding our family attended earlier in the day. My room smelled faintly of yesterday's church clothes; outside, laughter echoed like bells I wasn't invited to ring. Action figures were strewn about, preparing for another rescue mission. Softly, my friend, Mary appeared. She looked real, just like any other person I might come across. Thankfully, no one else could see her, so I didn't have to share her. I loved Mary.

"Hello, my silly friend," I said.

"Hello. Thomas. What are you doing?"

"I'm playing."

"What are you playing?"

"You know, our game." I replied. Rescue was a game of adventure, where action figures found themselves in perilous situations, and our job (mine and Mary's) was to save them from danger.

"I see. Is it fun?"

"Yeah, but it would be better if I had some friends to play with."

"Yes, I know. You'll have so many friends you won't even understand why, but you will have so many, Thomas."

"That sounds awesome. Have any idea when?"

"Yes, I do. It won't be for a bit, but you will be so happy. Can you imagine having more friends than you could possibly invite over for dinner?"

"No. I would be happy with just one or two friends at this point. I feel so alone. Could I have one of them now? Please?"

"No. It's not time. But you have me. We have each other."

"Yes, I know. But it's not the same." I said.

"Yes, I know, but trust me. You will have so much to enjoy in this life. Look to your future years with me. See what I see, feel what I feel. It's delightful."

"I don't think you understand. I want a friend. Please, find me a friend." I felt indignant.

Despite my pleading, she replied, "I can't do that. It's not time. But you will have many friends. I will be there when you do, and we will laugh at this moment."

I remember feeling so low. Nowhere to go. Defeated. Lost. You've heard a little of my story before I became known as a spiritual healer, but I didn't share this part. No one liked me.

Everyone looked at me and ran. I was alone. You have to know that's incredibly painful, and maybe you do. I suppose that's why I developed such a strong relationship with our Beloved. If I had been surrounded by friends at a young age, I wouldn't have had the time, I suppose. But I did have the time, and as I looked back, I appreciated the gift our creator gave me. Now that you've heard about Mary, I'll share a funny story that helps people rejoice and recognize their own beautiful life, often beyond comprehension.

Mary first came to me in dreams—always the same girl of light who called my name softly before dawn. In one dream, she motioned me over on the playground and said, "I'll come visit you soon." She was calm, gentle, and loving. Sometimes, I heard her waking me up, as if she were right there beside my bed calling my name, "Thomas, Thomas, Thomas. It's time to get up." Then on the Friday morning of my seventh birthday, while wide awake, the sunlight condensed, the air shimmered, and what had been a beam became a presence. Mary stepped from my dream-world into waking light. The room brightened the way water brightens when the sun touches it.

I had been listening to kids laughing outside, playing in the summer sun. Tears streamed down my face as I lay by my open window, hoping someday to have friends.

She appeared young at first. My age. Cute—just as she was in my dreams. I liked her curly brown hair, beautiful smile, and playful attitude. Like time-lapsed photography, she quickly grew before my eyes. Soon she was twenty-five or so, with shiny brown hair. Straight. Eyes of pure bliss.

She broke the silence saying, "Hey, Thomas. Would you like to play?"

"Who are you?" I asked.

"A friend of God," she said with love.

"I know you. I know your voice," I said. "You got so big!"

"It's still the same me. I've been visiting you every night and telling you I'd be here so as to not startle you."

She sounded just like she did in the dreams. She wore a tunic with a beautiful mantle over her head. Despite being made of pure light, it looked just like images I'd seen of Mother Mary.

"I am Mary. I've come to support you in developing a relationship with my serious nature, love. You are a man in a shallow body. This shallow body is needed. I have come to enlarge it and bring forth awareness of someone special to me. You know of whom I speak. He has come so that all may have love renewed in their lives. My Son has come to renew life, Thomas. He wishes to know you. But first, you might want to know who He is."

And then she began to speak about her Son, who was a fun boy and who had so much life in him. He reminded her of God, and so many people had persecuted him and ultimately put him to death.

"He was amazing," she said. "When He was a boy, like you, He told me about his mission, and I believed Him, for the Holy Spirit had already awakened me to His path. I care so much for Him as I do you. And when you realize how my love has transformed worlds, you will know I have come as a friend, and me as your friend is enough. Dry your eyes now, Thomas. You have a friend."

My new friend joyfully laughed and shared story after story; little boy stories initially. One of which was so amazing: Her Son was running after His friends. He ran into a bush and got twisted up, and He laughed. Mary saw this happen and was overjoyed watching Him cradled by the bush, like God catching Him in a big hug. She said, "Wait, don't get up yet. Let me take this in." Her heart, open with love, imprinted the image of her Son and a love for the bush that caught Him. The bush that was so wonderful to them over the years, providing berries and shade.

Years later, as she recalled the bush catching her Son, Jesus arrived and shared, "I won't be with you much longer, mother. I will wear the crown of the bush, and I want you to know I will wear it with the awareness that God has brought through me all that this life could bring. It's now time for me to transition to my next chapter, my next evolution, if you will." He told her that she was to carry forward her friendship with everyone who would seek Him and call Him brother; a brother in Christ.

"That's you," she said to me.

I did not know what she meant. She told me I would develop mastery in this world and invited me to say a prayer. I listened and repeated, "Amen, I say to you, I've come to live and learn and develop so that Christ may live in me." Then Jesus showed up—her Son.

Every night for a long time, He would invite me to go on a journey. I always accepted. Sometimes we would just sit in my room, and the journey was in my imagination. Other times we left, departing on adventures around the area.

Once, we sat at a creek. The moon trembled in the water as Jesus pointed to a rock and asked, "What is it that you see?"

"A rock," I replied.

"No. What is it about the rock that you see?"

A fear of getting it wrong surfaced. When panic flickered across my face, He placed a hand on my leg—steady, reassuring—and calm spread through me like ripples. I looked again and noticed there was a bug on top of that rock. Water rushed toward the rock and moved around it. The moon reflected in the water just beyond, and frogs sat at the edge of the water.

"I see that the rock sits among all sorts of life. I love the rock."

"Yes! See? You have seen the rock. God created that, and it is alive. It provides refuge for our little friend, quickens the water, and will someday be pulverized. Now, can you tell me what will happen to the rock upon being pulverized?"

I had no idea, of course, and replied, "No, what will happen?"

"You will find out. We will find out. We never know how life will emerge, but I do know they're planning a road, and they will use all the rocks they can to support creating a solid base. And that road will go right along this way. This rock will certainly be pulled into that project and support transportation for many years. What a wonderful existence!"

I tried to follow, but His words were oceans and I was still learning to swim.

He went on to say, "I had an amazing experience in my own life. Sometimes I taught people. Other times I laughed and played! What you might know of my story is my death and subsequent resurrection, but I say unto you, you have no idea who it is you speak of when you speak of my life. Were you there when I scooped up my cousin and giggled with her, joyfully lifting her into the air, saying, 'I love you. You are such a precious gift?'"

"No, of course not," I said.

"Were you there when I led my friends into new depths of awakening to the joys of who I was, who God is?"

"No, of course I was never there."

"Were you there when they told me my life was to end?"

I felt sadness. "No, I was not there."

"But, you were. You were there, Thomas. I didn't tell you this before, but I've known you forever. I know you remember and will know my name soon."

What was He talking about? I did know His name. I thought I did. Did He just say I was there? Was I Him? Was I Jesus?

Apparently, He sensed my struggle. "Your name is not Jesus. You are not me as your human mind perceives, but I live as you are, Thomas. Christ is alive in you. You will know more about this soon, but here's a fun concept. Imagine you were there in the beginning. You were known then, long before you ever formed this body. Now, you are occupying this body, just as you live in your home. Are you the home you live in?"

"No. I just live there."

"Right. Like that, you are not the body you occupy. You have chores at home, right?"

"Yes. I clean my room every Saturday, rake leaves in the fall, pick up grass clippings, clear dishes after meals, things like that.

"Why do you do these things, Thomas?"

"Because I have to. My mom and dad make me."

"Yes, they want you to learn to take good care of this beautiful home. If you didn't, it would fall into disarray. Likewise, you have a body as your spiritual *home* to occupy during this life. You must take care of your body well too. When you do, you will mature into your fulfillment at an early age. You will embody all that you are, bringing the fullness of your spirit to the earth. You see, Thomas, you have been known since the beginning. I'm referring to your Napsha, an Aramaic word that has no simple English translation. When you learn more about this, you will learn that at some level nothing has ever been that is not of you."

He paused to let that register, seeing my mental wheels spinning rapidly. Very little of it made sense to my ten-year-old mind, though the house metaphor helped. I stared blankly, processing until he interrupted, "Thomas, the fullness of your name is my name and will be one with my name for eternity. Your napsha is one with God." And that was that. I accepted it. What he said felt true, even if I didn't understand fully. "Rest now." He told me. "You are right where you need to be.

From that night forward, He came often—many dreams over many nights. Each journey built upon the last until the landscapes themselves began to recognize me. We traveled to villages and high places, distant lands, and unfamiliar dimensions. He brought me to teachers, and I learned about realities I was blind to before.

It was clear during our adventure that God works in awesome ways. Whether it's a person, caterpillar, or buffalo, God's life force flows through all beings, going well beyond our temporary encampment of life into infinite dimensions of grandeur and awe. The seed of expectation that our universe had to understand itself was deeply planted.

Jesus showed me how identification with the physical kept people focused on a temporary world, and cycles of trained circumventions blocked people from experiencing the essence of God. The theme of those dream lessons—expectations needed to be changed.

For example, he highlighted that I considered myself only as an individual, separate from others. He offered a different perspective. "Thomas, all on Earth are invited to care for each other. As more people do this, the active forces of God grow throughout humanity, opening up heavenly, dimensional pathways to new ideas, behaviors, technologies, and explorations that will look like magic tricks to today's population, but will be extraordinarily normal for future populations."

"Imagine the world functioning in perfection like a healthy human being—the heart, lungs, eyes, ears, mouth, cells… everything working harmoniously, supporting the life force of that individual. But if we poison that individual, the body and mind will deteriorate quickly. In the same way, I am showing you what is possible in a universe where people join together as they are designed to be, co-creating together with God in holy perfection."

I realized as Jesus spoke, this was what he meant when he said that I am Him. He was revealing living in a relationship as one, just as a body is one, but made up of many parts. Together, they function in sync, in harmony as one unit. Jesus suggested that that is the way of a purified world. We are to allow our individual parts to collectively function in alignment with our Creator and thus the totality of all. He assured me, if all people did this, there would be no wars—our planet would change.

Jesus then showed me a cartoon image of a person fighting themselves. Every time a punch landed, the person throwing the punch felt the pain of the one being punched. He added, "This is what people do when they are out of alignment, Thomas. They hurt themselves in attempting to harm another. If they knew the truth, they would not fight, but instead help from love. Wars are collectives of people attempting to change other collectives by force. Just like you see in the cartoon, it cannot work. It will never produce the outcome they desire."

"What should they do then?" I asked.

"They would be best to connect first with God. In doing so, they will be purified, and then see the light of God in others. Those who can maintain this presence of love as they look upon another will treat them accordingly. This is what I meant during my life when I said to love your neighbor as yourself, but first love God with your whole heart, soul, mind, and strength (Mark 12:30-31). When people purify, they transform and think differently. They align with and receive wisdom from the heavens.

The only way one can rise against another is if they are diseased, out of alignment and full of distorted thoughts—individually or collectively."

My journey came to an end when I woke up the next morning. Suddenly, my image of God, as a giant hanging out in the clouds, no longer felt true. My worldview had expanded beyond the edges of my imagination. I felt like I could fly—as if a new world of possibilities had opened. That morning I no longer prayed to reach heaven—I began to remember I had come from there. I wanted purification. And so, I began an inward journey, looking everywhere within me for God.

CHAPTER 6
PURIFIED ROOMS

The temple's outer court murmured below my perch; prayer held me still. What follows is one of the moments God used to move me from the boy of visions into the priest they now called on—a lesson that began inside and ripened into service.

As I looked for God, spiritual awareness naturally expanded, and my adventures with Jesus evolved to nourish my soul. Saint Teresa of Ávila described the soul as a diamond, like a crystal castle of many rooms or mansions: we begin outside the castle with noise, confusion, and distraction. We progress inward through darkness into light; to the center, where love burns clear. I wanted every room opened and searched, cleansed, and expressed in God's name. Hunger carried me forward.

By fourteen, I was practiced in this interior way. One cool spring morning, a woman I had never met stopped at our front steps. She was tall and thinned by trouble; her hair was jagged, her tunic stained. A sweetness of cheap perfume cut the clean air, and beneath it—something gone sour.

"My name is Eloise," she said through the screen, voice raw. "Last night a friend of mine dreamed of a boy named Thomas. A hand drew her a map in the dream. A voice told her to give me the map. I walked the roads. I don't know you. But I was told you would know what to do."

Training said: be still and allow God. Without planning it, words rose and carried their own weight. "In the name of the Father, and of the Son, and of the Holy Spirit—kneel." She did. The surprise flashed through me; I felt both small and held; covered in the precious blood of Jesus. "In the name of our Creator, any ill-willed spirits: leave this woman in the name of Jesus, the Holy Son of God. Amen."

Her jaw tightened; a guttural voice answered, "I have control here." Foam pearled at the corners of her mouth. I placed one foot forward so she could steady herself and said, "Put your forehead to my shoe." She bowed. "I command all ill spirits to come out of this woman and stand before God." Her body shuddered—first a tremor, then a violent shake—then loosened, and she rolled onto her side as gently as a child being rocked.

Inside, I heard: *You have a new gift. In the name of the Father has implications. You have ideas about what that means, and I expect you will hold on to those until the day they are cleansed. On that day, you will know why you say 'in the name of anything.' When you reach that day, you will command them as my son.*

Eloise blinked as though waking, eyes clear and wet. She looked bewildered and unaware of what had just happened. "How did I get here?"

"You were led," I said.

"Who are you?"

"You know who I am. A servant to God." I answered, and felt the truth of it; God had done this. She began to cry softly. "It's You," she whispered. "It's God."

I shook, confused at the situation. I wanted to pull her hands away and say, *No—don't clothe me with that.* If she clung to me instead of God, we'd only trade one prison for another. Even so, it did feel as if God had descended upon me, opened within me, and spoke, "I'm going to use you, and you're going to be a witness to this, but you are no longer who you are, but as I am."

I called my mom, who came quickly. She was initially frightened, for the woman was quite a ghastly sight. Eloise spoke, "Your son has healed me. I was possessed and am no longer. I've done things I hadn't wanted to, but felt compelled. Those urges are gone because of your son. You must teach him to know who he is."

I watched my mother's eyes flicker between us—fear, pride, confusion—all in the same blink. She had prayed her whole life; now those prayers were standing on our front step, muddy and breathing

Eloise continued, "There's a master I've heard of. I've never met him, but I hear he's a great teacher."

A little startled, my mother took a deep breath, digesting what the woman said before responding, "Thank you for your kindness. I would like to find this teacher for my son. Do you know his name?"

"I'm told his name is Yeeshatama, and that he is unfindable unless you are found. Go to the temple and ask for Rozeepa. She knows Yeeshatama."

"And what is your name?" my mother asked.

"I'm Rozeepa's daughter, Eloise. She'll be expecting you, for no one has been able to heal me until this moment. You will be known throughout the lands, Thomas." She looked at me with a sweet smile, despite the tears on her dirty face, her jagged hair, and her unkempt clothes. In that moment, all I saw was her light-body in holy union with our Creator, who clearly brought her to us. She opened my heart to something so new and awe-filled that I couldn't think; I could only feel sensations coursing throughout my body. Waves of energy, like ocean water, rolled from my head to my feet and back, shaking loose the *cobwebs* and illuminating the darkness. I felt the awesomeness of God.

The next day, my mother took me to find Rozeepa. She was sweeping the steps of a four-story temple: a rough cloak over her shoulders, slight hunch, a broom that looked older than the stones.

"Rozeepa?" my mother asked.

"Who's asking?" the woman said without looking up.

"Your daughter, Eloise, came to our home," I said.

Her head lifted. Years fell from her face as she hurried down the steps, catching my hands, the broom tucked under her arm for balance. "Thank you," she said, breathless. "You saved my daughter." Rozeepa had so much life in her, bouncing with delight. Her smile, framed by a dimple, reminded me of my fifth grade crush. It was quite a sight to see. I'd never been greeted that way—with such devotion, care, and wonder—but I was also experiencing wonder.

"Oh, you should see Eloise! She's a gorgeous woman. Just wait. You'll meet her again."

My mother, normally the one leading, stood behind, admiring the scene. Rozeepa led us down a corridor within the temple to a very large room, clearly set for a wedding or some type of ritual banquet. We sat at one of the tables as she questioned me.

"How did this happen? How is it that you knew what to do?" she pressed.

I took a breath and waited for an answer in my spirit. Why did I wait for an answer, you might ask? The experience with Eloise wasn't something I understood. It wasn't like a math problem I was trained to solve. Instead, I had learned to rest in an inner space, empty, devoid of content and thought—a place where I felt happy, fulfilled. There was a glorious resonant frequency with my soul. I didn't know how I got there, but I did recall the first time I visited. It reached out and spoke to me.

I had been praying and practicing what Jesus taught me—removing judgments, releasing the ideas I clung to about almost everything—emptying myself and resting in God's love, that perfect, freeing love. So real. So alive. Spontaneous joy bubbled up through me, tickling from the inside. My smile beamed on its own, widening as the joy rose. I can still tap into those feelings as I think about it. Incredible.

The joy turned to sorrow as undeserving thoughts crept into my mind: I didn't have a reason to be loved like that. Despite this thought, I wanted more, wishing I could bottle those feelings and share it with others.

Early on, I stayed in that space no more than five minutes before feeling nervous and running off to do something else. There was so much energy. I just had to move. But I learned to sit in it longer—ten minutes, then fifteen—until I could be in that space while doing the dishes or in a classroom at my school. Before I knew it, I was mostly in that space, rarely to be pulled away from it. Even those moments of disconnection were glorious, for they reminded me of where I still had something blocking God's love from fully being alive in me.

More time in that holy space came as I continued applying Jesus' practices: releasing control, regulating emotions, and letting go of perceptions I held dear. One of the most challenging perceptions to release was the idea that God was outside of me, watching from afar—an external witness to my life. I held onto this until my inner teacher invited me to temporarily let it go. In letting go, I discovered God alive in those bubbles of joy, in me. As I accepted God within me, things changed. For example, one day my mouth opened, and words poured out. I had no intention of speaking, but they flowed effortlessly. The words danced with laughter and love through a story that captured the room's attention.

It was like, "Here's me, do-di-do-di-do," and then I released the "me" I thought I was. In that space, the Divine spoke through me. God was no longer only out there in other parts of creation but was very much alive within me. As my voice became more aligned with God's voice, the separation of identity waned and weakened until the last vestiges of fear dissolved. I grew to sustain that experience regularly.

More and more, I saw God in others, and shared Jesus' teachings. Witnessing their experience of enlightenment was even more rewarding than my own. Their faces looked softer, gentler. Their eyes shone brighter. Heaviness in their hearts lifted. They looked younger. They hungered to know and serve God. The words Jesus first shared when I was ten had become my reality: connect with God, love your neighbor as yourself, and trust the process.

———

All that had prepared me for Eloise showing up at our door; prepared me…All that prepared me for Eloise showing up at our door; prepared me to witness the words flooding from my mouth with perfect intonation, command, beauty, and love; and prepared me to use a spiritual gift—the gift that would eventually lead military leaders to hire me to heal their wounded. This is the gift I was aware of as I sat with my mother and Rozeepa, wondering if I should share it with them.

Feeling uncomfortable, I clammed up. I was still just a boy. My mother returned me to that temple for three more weeks of visiting, assisting with chores, and sitting silently before Rozeepa changed her tack.

"Use the gift or lose it," she said. "Go to the hospital. Sit with the patients. Then tell me why you did what you did with each one." Part of me wanted to hide in the safety of prayer and dreams. Hospitals were full of fluorescent lights and failed hopes. But another part—the part God had been enlarging—leaned in. I looked at my mom. Our eyebrows lifted with shoulder shrugs to indicate, "Why not. Let's do it."

Each day I observed, took notes, and monitored patients. It was a small place—forty beds, white curtains, the smell of antiseptic and the latest tech creating a constant hum. I mostly listened. Sometimes an odd instruction arrived for someone: One day, I told a woman to walk down to the nourishment center, grab a biscuit, and step on it. She did and screamed. Nearby orderlies rushed to her, and she exclaimed, "I'm cured! I'm cured!" They couldn't explain it. She returned to thank me, associating my instruction with her healing.

Another woman was jumping up and down, and I told her to sing a nursery rhyme as she jumped. She began to sing and then crumbled to the floor in tears. Within a week, her skin healed from a multi-year affliction.

A man in a wheelchair charged at me like a bull. I said, "Stop," and he did. "Get on your knees and pray that you shall be taken into the heavens on chariots of fire." After he said the prayer, his legs, broken before, began to tingle and heal. I saw new blood vessels forming in my mind's eye, giving those broken legs new life.

As the results piled up, doctors invited me to join them while administering to patients. They did their thing. I mostly listened, but added insights when I could—only if they were real though.

What does "real" mean? In the early days, I got so excited that people healed in my presence that I tried to heal people myself. It never worked. It was a nice idea, but it wasn't God's way. God was the one doing the healing. I'll always remember that. God's way was also a mystery. I don't know how it even works today, to tell you the truth. Week after week, I returned to Rozeepa with incredible stories, and she would smile and say, "Good, go again next week."

Then Yeeshatama showed up; the master teacher Rozeepa's

daughter referred to. He looked just like the paintings I'd seen. Yeeshatama was about six feet tall, in his late 30s and looked like a king adorned with gold. He called to me as I left the hospital one evening.

"You there." I looked back and almost burst out laughing. He looked so out of place. His royal outfit shimmered with an opulent purple and gold robe, intricately embroidered with elaborate patterns and adorned with precious gemstones. A majestic crown, encrusted with diamonds and rubies, sat atop his head. It reflected the sun in a dazzling display of wealth and power. "You like my outfit, don't you?" he asked. My facial expression clearly revealed thoughts of how ridiculous he looked.

"That's quite an outfit. Where did you get it?" I asked.

He looked down and said with a smile, "Oh, this old thing?" Then he waved his hand above his head and swiped it down along the front of his body. As he did, his appearance changed to Jesus.

"What? You're Yeeshatama?"

"I suppose I am," he said, laughing. "It's good to see you, my friend." He grabbed me in a big bear hug, and I felt so loved.

"Why do they call you Yeeshatama?" I asked.

Jesus replied, "You'd be surprised what people call me, Thomas. But they do call. They always call." He laughed again. He was so happy, funny, and jovial. I liked him so much and felt blessed to be with my friend.

"Wait till I tell Rozeepa that her Yeeshatama is Jesus," I said excitedly.

He looked at me and said, "You can tell her, but she's not going to understand."

"Of course she will. Won't she?" I questioned my enthusiasm.

"They don't like Jesus here," he shared. "They had a situation in their temple where a woman claimed Jesus told her lies. She was angry about a personal situation and made the whole thing up. However, by the time truth surfaced, the momentum against

Jesus had snowballed. Generations later, they still don't accept him."

"But they're totally accepting of you. They're just calling you Yeeshatama. How did that happen?"

"More important than how it happened is that it did. If you look at all of their rituals and practices, don't they sound a little familiar?"

"Yes, I was thinking exactly that. But so few of their people actually practice the teachings. It's almost like they want to suffer."

"Yes! And as you know, suffering is optional."

I was reminded of a lesson of suffering Jesus shared during one of our first encounters. He said I could view rejection through the eyes of a victim and repeatedly feel the pain of suffering as an outcome from sowing those *seeds*. Or, I could embrace the suffering, drop my judgments, let go of how I saw things, and allow my perceptions to be corrected—seeing the possibilities God might be working through rejection. This helped me see my role in suffering—a wonderful awakening for me.

He had shared, "If you experience overcharged, heightened emotions, remember that reveals resistance in you. That resistance generates a powerful energy field begging for attention. God's holy universe is designed to support healing and dismantling these unhealthy *charges*, drawing to you what is optimal to address those hidden *gems*.

"You can trust what you attract in life to heal these charges and restore you to balance. Alternatively, you can resist and reject what you attract. That resistance, however, will block you from the truth and keep you stuck. Reconciling resistance opens pathways to God where new options and choices surface. If you do this, you will live in God—you will be the expression of love as you were designed."

That one lesson helped me heal tremendously; yet the whole Yeeshatama situation challenged me, revealing remnants of resistance still available to surrender. An entire community had rejected Jesus. He wasn't fazed by it, so why would it faze me? After all, it made sense, intellectually, to give them Yeeshatama, a way to connect with God after rejecting Jesus. Genius, really. Emotionally, though, God and Jesus were tied at the hip as one. I wanted everyone to know Jesus. Perhaps they still would someday. Through Yeeshatama, certainly they already did.

After encountering Yeeshatama—Jesus—I stopped trying to convince people to think how I thought, and instead sought to understand how they thought. I met them where they were on their journeys, using language that resonated best for them. Because of this, I learned to work with anyone, even those with no relationship to God.

While working with a broad variety of people on their relationship with self, God and all, I witnessed firsthand how universally effective the healing principles were. Though the world provided context for people, the true healing happened in the spirit. The principles were simple, yet resistance could prove difficult for people's willingness to complete their training. Many had a single moment of awakening and felt they were complete, abandoning the principles as if one exercise was enough. However, those who stuck with them were blessed with full transformation, a transformation that resulted in conscious union with God, their Source of life, power, love, joy, all of it.

This process included the death and rebirth of many *parts* within them. Remember I said I was trying to heal people? That *part* of me, for example, died and re-emerged integrated—accepting that I was not the one doing the healing. God did all of it. Fighting God for control, my old unconscious strategy, was no longer an option. As time went on, I grew to believe people can live 100% in tune with God. My teacher in that process was Jesus, or Yeeshatama to friends living near the temple.

That season taught me this: anything can be healed. People are like knotted yarn; God knows where to loosen a single loop so the whole snarl yields. God guided me to support the unraveling of people's drama and issues, strengthening their trust in God. Of myself, I had no capacity to help. It was only through the Beloved's presence that I was of any use.

Human beings are such interesting creatures—we get all balled up and have no idea how we even got tangled. It could have started before we were even incarnated. Anything that is an obstacle to our sustained pure state of consciousness must be revisited, collapsed, and retrained. Our part is willingness.

The court below my perch stirred, cots shifting, voices rising. My work there was simple to name and endless to practice: help souls grow aligned and sturdy spiritual bodies, teach them to live in God's current, remind them that love is stronger than the stories that hold them captive. I was God's *soldier* and felt at home in my post. I was back.

CHAPTER 7
SO... I FOUND HEAVEN

onths had passed. The war ground on, but life in the temple had taken root. My newfound zest for my role served me and everyone well. Long gone was my disdain for Pablo and the others. I no longer viewed myself as being imprisoned in a war camp, but instead I was completely free. This adjusted attitude helped me help others more effectively as the war persisted.

New awareness of what was taking place emerged over time. My role, according to military leaders, was physical restoration, but God's plans went well beyond the physical. On a cool Tuesday morning in July, I gathered everyone in the outer temple ring. Amidst the many fresh faces were those still on the mend. That morning I shared a concept inspired by dozens of reports reinforcing the unusual healing experiences at our hospital.

One young woman in particular reported how her left ankle miraculously healed and she felt guilty. She couldn't stop thinking of those who had died before reaching our hospital—survivor's guilt.

Her story, echoed by others, led me to pray: *What happens when our soldiers don't make it?* After all, war is brutal, and there's only so much that can be done. I couldn't help everyone—God couldn't stop every death. Even those who made it to our hospital didn't all survive. That haunted me. If heaven was real, where were they now? Had I failed them? Had God?

Having regular conversations with God led to that communication channel being as quick as talking with someone physically in the room. First, God informed me that not all people could receive the healing gift, sometimes due to their own blocks.

Though it might not have helped everyone, I felt an urgency to share God's wisdom. I informed people that God wasn't withholding healing, and their changes internally could accelerate any healings possible for them.

That's a delicate subject, of course. Many thought of themselves as victims, and rightly so—they were blown up, shot at, and dismantled in a variety of horrifying ways. Those who didn't have physical injuries were traumatized in mental and emotional ways. So how did I convey that such a helpless-looking set of circumstances could possibly be within their power to influence? As the group gathered, I came down from my perch. Though I could see well, I didn't like that it looked like a pedestal I was placed upon. I was not any greater or less than any of them, and I wanted them to feel that. As they found their places and the room quieted, I shared one of my favorite stories heard in childhood.

Once upon a time," I started, "there was a huge massacre on an island off the coast of Hawaii. Hawaii is a series of islands, but this one had no inhabitants until a shipwreck stranded fourteen soldiers. Some began making a shelter while others gathered firewood and searched for food. But one was aggressive. He wanted everyone to do what he wanted, and when people didn't listen, he grew loud. His face got beet red as he flailed about trying to get people to listen. Completely out of touch, people moved away from him saying things like, "Get lost", "Knock it off", and "This isn't helpful, Randy". As pressure mounted against him, he lost it, ravaging everything, taking supplies, and departing. Thankful for his departure, the others worked as a team, each contributing their unique skills to survive the shipwreck.

"While isolated, Randy sulked, shouted, and called out, 'God, if you can hear me, then you know we've crashed, and you must send help.' He said that regularly, blind to the 13 others who were doing just fine given the conditions. He stayed as far as possible from them, thinking they didn't like him or value him.

"He foraged daily in the morning, eating whatever he could, but occasionally ingesting something that made him ill. He would then pray, 'God, if you are there, heal me from this ailment.' God would look down and say, 'You realize there are 13 other people on this island who would be happy to support you.' But the man was so loud in his discouragement that he failed to hear God's words. Attempting to get messages to the isolated man, God offered insights through dreams, animals, and the forces of nature. They all fell on deaf ears and blind eyes.

"One day, Randy slipped and fell into a very deep hole. Trapped, unable to lift himself out, he cried, 'God, you can't possibly let your child die this way.' God looked down, smiled, and saw that His child was going through such a massive struggle. The man's choices created such a tormenting situation that God thought it was quite an amazing creation of self-destruction. Needless to say, God spoke to the other 13 who were in a spirit of life, love, and joy despite their circumstances. It came as an insight to seek food in a new area. The thirteen listened, forged new paths, climbed high and low, and eventually found food, and heard whimpering.

"Following the sound, they came upon the hole, looked down, and asked, 'Is that you, Randy?' He looked up, embarrassed that they found him in such a weakened state. Getting him out of the hole was easy; keeping him alive was a challenge. But they did it, bringing him back to their camp and nourishing him for three days.

"Eventually, Randy's fever broke, and as he swam in the ocean, he called out, 'God, why did you make me so weak? Why was I so dependent on these other people, people I hate? Yet they've shown me such mercy and compassion after I treated them horribly. I know not what to do. Guide me, please.'

Just then an eagle swooped down with a high-pitched whistle, and miraculously rested its talons on the water. Something happened as Randy stared into the eagle's eyes, and he heard a voice break through the noise of his mind, simply saying, 'I love you.'

Filled with joy and smiling, he asked, 'Why would you do this to me, God?'

He didn't hear God's answer; he was too lost in the exhilaration of hearing, "I love you."

Finished with the story, I turned to those gathered and said, "This story illustrates your situation. I know you didn't ask to be here; none of you signed up to be shattered. You perceive yourselves as victims of those who waged war, or of enemies who inflicted wounds. Yet, by looking at yourselves through the eyes of victimhood, you block the intelligence of God that would otherwise be available to you. You think you have come here to heal, but will have healed nothing if you walk away with your once broken arm made whole. Instead, let God's love restore all your parts, and renew a relationship that will go beyond the physical. Allow the heavens to be revealed now and wherever you might go."

Though most left, uninterested in pursuing it further, a few wanted more. They would meet me as often as possible, for hours at a time. One of them soon asked, "My teacher, can I share something that happened to me? I'm caring for myself and others as you said, but it's so strange."

"Of course," I replied. "Please continue."

He came closer and cautiously whispered, "An angel appeared before me. She said that I was to go and create a dynasty that would care for God's creatures. What does it mean?"

I laughed and asked, "What does it mean to you?"

"Well, I guess it means that I'll get married someday, have offspring, and they will run zoos or something of this nature. Is that possible?"

"I do not know if that is going to happen," I said. "However, you can trust that if an angel came to you and shared this, it is likely to happen. In fact, in some cultures, they would say it has already happened; you just haven't experienced it yet."

Curious, he asked, "Whatever do you mean 'already happened'?"

"Well, a part of you has experienced your future, or potential future. You can accept it and act aligned with that vision or not. If an angel comes to you, then you must either be on the right path, or you're being shown the right path. You've been given a great gift—encouragement, perhaps. But it won't necessarily look how you think it will. It will be what it is at that time, but the vision is alive, and that's the trajectory of your optimal life, at least a direction for now. While so many people spin in circles, you have clear sight. Now, in prayer, ask if there's anything more to be aware of at this time."

The man looked away and asked, "God, is there anything more to be aware of now?" He waited, then lit up and said, "Oh my! Teacher, I got an answer!"

"What is it?" I was eager.

"I'm to leave here at once and go south. I will meet my bride on my way to my destination."

Is your destination clear?" I asked.

As if he were looking at it in his mind, he said, "I see a map and a pin that's right in the middle of Islam land."

"Islam land? Where is that?" I asked.

"It's what I call it. I don't know the actual name, but that's what my ancestors called it. I will go there."

It wasn't long before his things were packed and he left. Before he did, he came to say goodbye and asked, "Is this heaven?"

I had never been asked that question before, but I supposed that this was as close to heaven as I had ever been. Oneness with God, seeing joy in the midst of such a horrid situation—perhaps this was heaven. I prayed and wrote quite a bit after the man departed, asking that question: *Hey God, is this heaven?*

And with that question, a miraculous experience unfolded before me. My eyes lifted to the ceiling, as if they wanted to roll back into my head. My eyelids fluttered and suddenly shut so tightly that I could hardly bear it. The darkness behind my eyelids gave way to a beautiful scene in space. I saw, not with my physical eyes, but with an inner vision— a universe so incredible and vast. A square wave of red, warm energy floated up to me. It was warm and then hot, as if I had entered a dry sauna. Though visually in space, I was still physically in that outer circle of the temple.

After the heat, I *traveled* to a new location where orbs of blue light moved about. It wasn't like I moved my legs; but was transported rapidly with no effort. The blue lights were cool and calming. Then I traveled again, passing planets. One of the planets got larger and larger until I was ultimately whisked inside. There, I saw people—large giants—gathering and speaking.

They clearly noticed me but ignored me at first. I sat and watched what felt like a ceremony. One of the giants began to speak, and as he did, his tales of adventure from outside the planet's center projected into the space around us like living images. I was enthralled, as if the stories were not stories at all but memories. Could they be? I wondered. What, exactly, was I witnessing?

The first giant's story was about a village of ants the size of rhinoceroses building a castle. Inside the castle were tiny people cared for by the *ants*. The people never saw the ants, thinking that God was creating something for them, as it all happened in the dead of night. The castles kept getting more glorious. We all saw this as the giants' imaginations holographically projected in our midst as they spoke. The ants were amazing builders, and the tiny humans were in awe of the magic of creation happening around them.

Another giant stepped forward with a second story, about water that grew into giant forms shaped like elk and they battled for gamesmanship, entertainment. It was spectacular to hear and see all of it.

While I eavesdropped on their conversations, one of the giants finally turned, looked straight at me, and asked, "Are you getting all of this?" I nodded, not really knowing what to say. As soon as I acknowledged that I got it, I was whisked away back to space.

Millions of stars lit up the atmosphere. A wave of blue light blocked some of the stars and shimmered toward me. It was cool and comforting at first, becoming chillier as it got close. I was moved again, right up to a throne. An amazing, brilliant, person-shaped light radiated from the throne. It was the brightest light I had ever seen, yet I could look right at it. It was gentle, kind, full of love. I was mesmerized, drawn into it.

A face then appeared in the chest of the first light. It was my friend, Jesus. His light-filled face was glorious. Despite this, I perceived facial features, hair and even a beard—all made of light. He smiled and then his face withdrew a bit back into the main body of light. A new shape, made from the same light, then came forth. It traveled out of the main body toward me, closer and closer. Finally, it entered me, resonating love throughout my cells. I experienced God's love, and said, "This is it, isn't it? This is heaven."

"Yes," a voice came from an unknown place, from every place.

"Who's speaking to me?" I asked.

"It is I. I am as I am. We are here to share the good news that you have indeed found heaven. What do you think so far?"

"I haven't seen much of it, I suppose, but I feel incredible. I've never felt this way before."

"Imagine whatever it is that you'd like, and it will be."

"I imagine a world where war comes to peace."

"And it shall be so," said the voice. "But not necessarily when you think it will. Trust that peace is coming; it's on its way. Remember me and this moment."

"But I want it now. Why can't we have it today?"

"If I were to tell you the answer, would you believe me?"

"I think I would believe just about anything you say at this point." After all, it did seem remarkable that I was transported to a place where our Creator, our Beloved, spoke to me so fluidly.

"I will tell you then. It will happen when the leaders of your world lay down their weapons and say, 'We've had enough. We won't get our way by doing what we have done. We shall think no more, and instead allow God's love to teach us.'"

I scoffed, "But that will never... Wait, are you saying..." I caught myself doubting, took a breath and started again, "Okay. When will that be?" I finally got the words out. Just because I saw our world being far from peace, didn't mean it couldn't happen. I just couldn't imagine a leader doing what God said, at least not in my lifetime. *God would have to force them*, I thought. Yes, force them. I wanted to share this idea, and did.

"Why don't you force them? Make them. They would have to do it then, wouldn't they?"

"Why would I do that? I created you to have free will. But I assure you, your leaders will one day awaken to the truth and invite me into their hearts. Change will come, and on that day, you will have your wish."

"Can I tell them what you told me?" I asked.

"Sure. You can share this entire conversation if you like. There may only be a few to hear your message, but please, I welcome you sharing it with the leaders. Let them know I'm waiting."

We looked at each other, my eyes on the prize in front of me, lost in God's amazing love. The one who spoke communicated telepathically, so I instantly received answers to all my questions, often before they were asked. I knew. I knew it was Him, God almighty, the creator of heaven and earth, of all that is seen and unseen. God was communicating with me!

I look back on that moment now and laugh at my naivety. I could have asked anything, and I wasted it just sitting there. Yet even now, I'm not sure asking for plans would have been wiser than simply being consumed by love. I was lost in awe. I saw that God knew we would eventually get there, though it didn't change my desire for things to be different.

War is so ugly. Where do people go when they die in war? I hope it's where I visited. I hope it's exactly where I went, for whatever happens in that place... it's good. So I found heaven. Now what would God have me do with it here?

CHAPTER 8
SEEING GOD

Back on my perch in the outer ring of the temple, the spirit of God stayed with me after my inquiry of heaven, accelerating the unwinding of errors holding me hostage to the world. My need to fix things in order to be liked fell away.

A settling came to my spirit; comfort, and wisdom in my life like never before. I felt different—centered and confident. God taught me to more fully support the gifts of the Spirit in myself and others. God said I would see the wisdom of humanity if I discarded the scraps and branches that had died years ago and focus on where life existed. I did this, focusing on the good, and feeling grateful for what I had; what we had. From that moment on, I was gentler, more aware, and alive in a way that felt natural, but out of this world. It might not make perfect sense, but that's how I felt. Something had changed. I felt purified and new.

Day after day, wounded bodies and restless souls were carried beneath my perch. My hands tended injuries; my words tended hearts. Following this, God asked me to share a story with every person who came into the temple from that day forward:

"When God is revealed to you, you will know it. You will see things changing. People will communicate with you in ways that bring you closer to God. But if you ignore, if you choose to hide, you can resist, but you can't resist without consequences. If I block a plant from budding out of the depths of its earthly home by placing a structure that blocks the light, there is a consequence. That plant is forced to find a way outside of the structure to receive light, or else that plant will not thrive. Who are you to block the love of God's holy light and prevent your divine destiny from coming forth? And why would you resist that? You may have a story that says you were harmed as a child and need to protect yourself. You may have a story that you don't deserve the love of God. You may have a thousand and ten stories and fear God's retribution because someone told you that you wouldn't stand a chance before God. But I'm here to tell you that's untrue. God is love, and in truth, I share with you that all judgments and consequences are just. Running from them benefits no one and delays what would inevitably occur anyway, which is healing, loving restoration, purification. You may not want purification for fear that you wouldn't be able to live and have the experiences you've become accustomed to. And that is the real sin: clinging to your own perception of right and wrong. What if you were to allow your perceptions to change? Will you come into the presence of God at this moment, join this ceremony, and allow God to touch upon wounds you've hidden and protected for your perceived safety? Will you let God in?"

Inevitably, people upon hearing this would either say yes or no. But once in a while, questions emerged. For example, "What is it that I'll have to do?" This is a common one, and it can come with fear. What if you are prompted to move across the country and do things differently than you have for the last 40 years? Wouldn't that be awful? These questions are natural. They don't usually have answers. To give yourself to God is to support yourself going through a metamorphosis. Then you will get your own answers directly from the Source. The fear of the unknown is one of the biggest reasons people remain stuck. It is necessary to take this seriously and act.

Though I told people they have the capacity to transform, many didn't believe me. It was like talking to bricks for a while. Some who came through the temple knew God only as a distant rule-maker. Others had found Yeeshatama. Some had heard Jesus' name mainly as a threat — the judge who watched and waited to punish. A few had no words at all, only a raw ache and a sense that *Someone* might still be listening. Wherever they started, God met them there.

I learned to enroll people patiently. Even if uncomfortable they took more action. Transformations quickened. Innate spiritual gifts unlocked in people. This happened more and more. Here are three simple examples of how that occurred:

JOSIE

Josie was a communications specialist. She feared putting herself in harm's way and hoped that her fellow soldiers would protect her. In an explosion, shrapnel bolted her arm to her head. This brought her to me. She wanted so badly to hide that she wouldn't even let me look at her wounds. She kept her gaze on the floor, shoulders caved in around the pain, as if her whole body were apologizing for existing. I gave her a simple prayer to say daily: "God, I let go of my own way and allow myself to open to yours."

Two weeks later, she slunk into the main room and came to the foot of the perch, moving carefully so each step wouldn't jostle her arm.

"Master teacher, I have a confession to make," she said, eyes still lowered. "I prayed your prayer every day, and I am aware that I don't want to go into battle. I'm afraid."

"Good," I replied, relieved she had come. "Stand up tall and look at your hands."

"You know I cannot do that," she said. "My arm's still stuck to my head. It is incredibly painful."

"I see. And you won't let anyone help?"

Her jaw clenched. "I don't deserve the help. As my soldiers bravely encountered the enemy, I hid. But even hiding didn't keep me safe."

I softened my voice. "I forgive you for this, and know that you're free of judgments in my presence."

Her eyes snapped up, searching my face. "How is that possible?" she asked.

"It is not my place to judge. The only right judgment is of God."

"And what is right judgment?" she asked.

"It is right to notice that you had fear and made a choice from that, which was your error. Right judgment points that out. Correcting that is to address the fear. Would you like to address that now?"

She hesitated, breath shallow. "I suppose. What would I have to do?"

"There is a simple prayer I'd like you to sit with. Is that something you're willing to do?"

"I suppose."

I wrote out this prayer for her, watching her injured hand tremble as she reached to take the paper:

"You have seen me hiding, and yet you still seek to have a relationship with me, God. I release trying to find ways to hide from you. I release trying to find ways of sinking down into a place where I think you won't see me. I cancel all of my needs to find you in the darkness. And I release trying to control how it is that I will have freedom from my fears. I ask that you lead the way. Amen."

"Go and pray for this," I concluded gently, "and return when you're ready."

Four weeks to the day, Josie returned. Her arm had released from her head, and she looked to be healing nicely. The shrapnel had been removed, and bandages encircled her head and arm. This time, her shoulders were a little higher, her steps more sure. She looked clean and alive, smiling.

"You look happy," I said.

"I feel different," she replied. "It's as if something weighing heavily on me no longer has weight. I am concerned it will come back, but at this moment, I feel free."

"And what was it that was weighing on you, my friend?"

She took a breath, the words catching in her throat. "I had this fear that Jesus was going to kill me. That's how they talked about Him when I was little—like a sword waiting to fall."

"Wow," I said softly. "Quite a story you told yourself. Why did that story have weight for you?"

She told me how Jesus had come to her and said she had to allow for God in everything, and everything unlike God must die. She assumed she was evil and that Jesus would take all the things that made her—her, the parts she judged as evil—and kill those things, leaving nothing behind.

In praying, God showed her that what Jesus actually does is guide people to awareness, such that God's holy purification process can gently come and lead someone home. This does require a metaphorical death process, but literally, there is still the core of life that must live. That is eternal. She freed herself by opening to God, and divine grace showed up, actually freeing her.

JOSIAH

Unlike Josie, Josiah wanted people to kill him. He believed he *should* die. When he came to me, he nearly had—his body half-gone with shock, his spirit clinging by a thread. Only a miraculous healing kept him here. When he recovered enough to speak, he asked me to help him let go of his desire to die.

He stood before me, thin and trembling, his eyes the dull color of ashes.

"What would happen if you died?" I asked softly.

"I'd be in heaven," he replied without hesitation.

"So if you die, you'll be in heaven?"

"Yes." His voice cracked. "Everything in my life is hard. If I were in heaven, I wouldn't feel so much struggle. I'd be with God. Everything would be better."

I asked God before responding, *Why does this person want to die?*

The answer came swiftly, like a whisper pressed into my chest:

He doesn't know how to address his pain. He wants a way out.

"What shall I do?" I asked silently.

"Tell him I love him," God said. "I've always loved him, and he will be freed from this."

"How do I do that? What words do I use? I surrender. Guide me."

A shift came over me—my concern eased and was replaced by an inner clarity, as though I were merely lending my throat to a message.

"Josiah," I began, "God says to tell you that you're going to go through a huge challenge. It's so big that most people could never understand how you will move mountains the way you will. But there is one thing you must accept in order to accept this challenge: you must receive His love. Are you willing to do that? Are you willing to receive God's love?"

He shook his head. Shame clouded his face. "I can't. I'm not worthy of it. I've sinned. I could never stand before God. At my core, I'm bad."

"So," I said gently, "you've decided you won't let Him love you because you see yourself as undeserving?"

He blinked, startled by his own logic. "That sounds... silly hearing you say it. Why wouldn't I let Him try to love me, even as bad as I am? But how would I do that?"

"Let go of your story," I said. "Simply call out:

'God of Heaven, I surrender myself to You.

I don't believe I deserve love or healing,

but I'm willing to receive it if it's Your will.

I release trying to tell You what to do.'"

He repeated the prayer, voice shaking, and then collapsed to his knees. His head bowed so low it nearly touched the floor.

Silence filled the room.

Then—softly, unbelievably—a tiny creature scurried forward. A mouse. It stopped before him, sniffed, then ran in three slow circles, as if marking a sacred boundary. Finally, it stood up on its hind legs, brought its tiny paws together, and bowed its head.

Josiah let out a sound somewhere between a gasp and a sob.

With trembling hands, he placed his palms together and whispered, "Thank you."

The mouse climbed onto his lap and settled there as though blessing him.

A warmth spread over Josiah's face—a dawning recognition of goodness.

"Maybe I *am* worthy," he whispered. "Maybe we all are. God... if I am unworthy, please make me worthy. I'm willing."

He closed his eyes, prayer rising from him like incense. When he looked back at me minutes later, something in him had returned—light, breath, presence.

"Thomas," he said, steady now, "I want to stay. I want to know God right here where I am."

Witnessing Josiah's healing renewed my own devotion. I

silently reiterated my desire to remain in the temple as long as God willed. If I lived my whole life healing soldiers in this place, that would be enough.

MELANIE

Melanie had served in the healing wing of the temple far longer than most. She moved through the room like sunrise—quiet, warm, unfailingly present. Her smile could soften even the most battle-hardened arrival. When she passed, people straightened, breathed easier, remembered themselves.

One afternoon, between waves of wounded soldiers, I asked her how she was always so cheerful.

Her answer startled me.

"I don't know how to describe it," she said, eyes shimmering with a truth she had carried for years. "You help people see what needs to be forgiven. God gave me something different."

She took a slow breath.

"I was told to *send God into every person who walks through these doors*. God is sent through my eyes. Every moment I'm with someone, I pray, 'God, let Your light shine into this one.' Not only the people who come seeking help. Anyone who thinks of me. Anyone who remembers me. Even those with harm in their hearts."

She looked down at her hands—gentle hands, steady hands. "People think they're reaching for *me*. But it's not me they want. Their brokenness is reaching for the God I carry."

"That is remarkable, Melanie. Were you always this way?" I asked.

She shook her head, a shadow moving through her expression.

"No," she said quietly. "When I was a little girl, I was unhappy. Men in my village abused me. I felt trapped, used, alone. When everyone left for work, I was left behind—'helping,' they said. But they took what they wanted."

Her voice didn't tremble. It was almost more heartbreaking that it didn't.

"One day," she continued, "I climbed behind my dresser looking for a lost earring and found my mother's prayer necklace. It had fallen into the pages of an ancient book. When I opened it, it taught me about God."

She lifted her chin slightly, recalling the moment.

"I prayed, *'If there's a real God out there, then let God enter everyone I see, so they won't need me or reach for me.'*"

She paused.

"That day, I stopped running. I stopped hiding. I allowed God's love to go *ahead* of me. And no one laid a hand on me again."

Sometimes her eyes glistened when she recalled those years, but this time she spoke with strength, not sorrow.

"Once in a while," she said, "a dark presence walks through these doors—someone carrying shame or rage. It's heavy. But in those moments, I double down: *'God, I can't do this. Go before me. Shine Your light in this person. Let them see You in me.'*"

Then she laughed softly. "And sometimes a slap to the hand or a needle jab helps them reset their attention. But always—always—I trust God to protect me."

I admired her deeply. Many who suffered abuse walked with slumped shoulders, heavy breath, eyes trained to the floor. Melanie carried no such weight. The memories lived in her, yes, but she refused to build a home for them. She placed her whole attention on God—and God bloomed through her like a field of morning light.

The more she focused on that Presence, the more people healed in her company. Not because she was extraordinary, but because she allowed God's extraordinariness to flow unblocked.

These three people—Josie, Josiah, and Melanie—demonstrate how God's love brings about change and allows for gifts and talents to come online, benefiting themselves and others. It's just so incredible.

Though God also started to teach me how to see Him in all the people, it was not always easy. One day, He called me into His "office" and reprimanded me. I was told, "If you focus on the evils in people, your insight will be clouded with darkness. Instead, look for the Christ in people. Look for Me. Once you see Me, keep your eyes on Me while allowing anything and everything to surface in your mind. This will clear a path for people to get unstuck. You have the capacity to choose love, forgiveness, and wholeness in this way."

"How does it work?" I asked.

"Let's pretend that you were going to a river to catch fish. Perhaps you have a fishing pole and a hook. Another person may cast a net. What I would love for you to do is recognize the fish as I recognize them. Instead of a pole or a net, say, 'Come to me,' and they will dance upon the water to listen to your words. Use that approach. That is the way I am asking you to teach. So get off this perch you comfortably sit upon and go out into the wilderness. Find the people at war, and call out to them, call their names, and they will listen."

"You want me to leave? I left once, Lord, and that didn't go so well."

"Trust. This time you'll leave with me."

"I feel nervous. There are so many questions. How will I know which of the people to call out to? And, what do I call them?"

"You'll know. And call them 'friend'."

CHAPTER 9
WHERE THE DYING RISE

The next day, I packed a knapsack and found the Active Director, Juneau, in charge of the facility.

"I want to leave and work with the soldiers before they're injured," I declared boldly. "If I can get to the field, I can train our soldiers to be more alert, on top of their emotions, centered, and more capable than they are now."

"That's foolish, Thomas. Even if what you say is true, why would you put your life at risk when you're doing such great work here?"

"Because, Juneau, that's where I'm needed most."

Believing me—but not liking it—she said I could go, but insisted I needed a soldier by my side for protection. I obliged.

Soon we had our backpacks and light sleeping arrangements ready, but I sensed something was off about the soldier assigned to accompany me. He didn't come off as super bright and appeared unusually enthusiastic to go to the front lines. When I brought the matter to Juneau she flatly stated, "Private First Class Jenkins is the one. Take him with you. Or you can stay here."

An inner voice reassured me that although he wasn't the soldier I imagined, he was the right man for the job. I accepted the situation and said my goodbyes to the temple staff.

Despite being offered transport, I chose to walk, trusting my intuition. PFC Jenkins and I left the temple on the four- to five-hour hike to our destination.

After ten minutes of silence, I started a conversation. "What do I call you, friend?" I asked.

Turning his head toward me, he replied, "Johnny. My name's Johnny."

"Where are you from?"

"Biloxi, Mississippi."

Johnny was tall, an imposing figure with bulging forearms and a steely demeanor. His blonde hair, kept in a tight military cut, framed piercing blue eyes. Johnny's rugged face, marked by battle, gave him a gruff, no-nonsense appearance. He looked like a typical man's man, strong and unwavering, taking orders only from his superior. Johnny's presence commanded respect and would instill a sense of fear in those who might dare cross us. My only fear was that he might shoot first and ask questions later. That's not what I was out here for.

"Johnny, I need to ask you a few questions. We need to be aligned on something."

"The only alignment I have is with my boss. I'm here to keep you alive. That's enough for me." He fell silent.

Shortly after, I tried again. "Johnny, there's something you need to be aware of before we go where we're headed. You need to pay attention and listen."

"All right, I give. What's so important?" he asked.

We walked side by side, his firearm slung over his shoulder, as we were still far from hostile territory. With no threats in the vicinity, he took out a breakfast bar, began eating, and looked at me, waiting.

Recognizing he was finally listening, I continued, "There's a person we're going to meet on this trip. He was shown to me in a dream. He has a long, pristine ponytail and looks exquisite. He's not our friend. I'll speak to him first, but be ready to apprehend him if needed. If it goes well, there will be no need for force. Do you understand?"

"You're telling me that you dreamt about a threat, believe it's going to happen, and I'm just supposed to let you walk into this danger? No way. How do you know this dream is accurate, anyway?"

He was rightfully cautious and understandably skeptical, but I had to get through to him. "I have a special relationship with God, and He warns me of things like this—prepares me. It has happened many times. I promise you, this is going to happen. I need you to be ready."

"Okay. If I play along and believe you for argument's sake, why not just let me capture him and tie him up first? That would prevent any possibility of harm, right?"

"Yes, that would keep us safe. However, he won't tell us the message he has if you do that. He'll clam up. Then the probability of you killing him will go way up before we get the intelligence. Please, let's do it my way. Can we agree on this?"

"Yes, but if he even flinches toward a weapon, he's gone," Johnny said firmly. "Can we agree on that?"

"Agreed," I said, needing Johnny to do his job, yet allowing this conversation to take place.

The silence that followed let both of us process what lay ahead. The only sounds were our pant legs swishing and gravel under our boots. After a while, I broke the silence with more details.

"Johnny, we're going to meet this person at a chapel in the next town."

Dismissing my forecast, Johnny said, "There's no way Pony-tail could get this close to our camp, sir."

"And yet, he has," I rebutted. "It's where we'll find him."

Seeing my conviction—perhaps feeling it—Johnny took his rifle off his shoulder and walked on alert, scouting the landscape from side to side.

The narrow road led toward a few dilapidated buildings in the distance. Unlike the barren land around the temple, we were surrounded by a vast expanse of wild grasses and flowers. Some of the grasses rose to shoulder height, most to our waists. A few trees dotted the landscape, touching a dull gray sky heavy with the promise of rain.

The gravel road transitioned to cracked asphalt. The town would be just around a bend, less than a mile up the road. The silence became almost oppressive, broken only by the rustle of nature in the gentle breeze and our footsteps.

An old gas station lay waste just outside of town. The wild fields were more trimmed here, kept shorter the closer we got. Rain fell just as we reached main street.

Our destination, the chapel, was visible well before we arrived. People milled about as we walked up the street. It was like something out of an old western. We passed the saloon, bank, a hotel and diner. Even the sheriff's office looked like a prop on a movie set.

At the end of the street, we entered the chapel. A lone man knelt near the altar. His back and ponytail faced us. Johnny looked at me with raised brows, acknowledging we had found the man from my dream. We stood quietly in the back, waiting for the gentleman to turn around.

"You can come up here if you like," he said, still kneeling. His voice boomed through the tall ceilings. Johnny and I walked gingerly to the front, Johnny taking the lead.

"What is your name, friend?" I asked.

"Timberwolf. I have a message for you, sir," Timberwolf said.

"What is it?"

"Your son here is huge. Do you need him, or can he wait outside?"

"Johnny is not my son, and he'll stay here."

"I assure you no harm will come to you. I know if it did, Johnny would certainly find retribution easy. So, I ask again, can he wait outside?"

I nodded to Johnny to head to the door. Reluctantly, he took a position where he could still see Timberwolf but could no longer hear.

"So, what's the message?" I asked.

"You're to go to the river north of the battle. You'll find safe passage along the riverbed. They just fought there last night, and it's been cleared out except for three huts. In the middle hut, there is a gentleman who has been wounded. I told him you would be coming. If you help him, it may just end this war. You won't get too close before being confronted. Tell them that Timberwolf sent you, and Johnny won't be able to go into the tent. If you can help this man, people will follow you."

"And if I can't help him?"

"Then you shouldn't go."

Timberwolf stood, shook my hand, and walked out.

Johnny didn't like the plan at all. He feared heading into enemy territory. I said he wouldn't have to—I could go alone. He didn't want that either. It was a conundrum.

This was a major change in plans, from finding our troops to walking straight toward the enemy. He feared letting his boss down. What if I were injured and no longer able to support our soldiers' healing? He wrestled with it, his loyalty clashing with something deeper stirring.

"I understand your concerns," I said, "but if this truly is the path that can end the war, how can we ignore it?"

He stared at the floorboard, jaw tight.

Then he said, "I remember when my parents were young, they took us to a wildlife park. We were in these covered trucks, driving past animals at a distance. At one point, the convoy stopped suddenly. A lion had escaped its enclosure. Rangers came, radios crackling, and told everyone to stay in the vehicles. There was talk of evacuating the park section by section.

"Our guide pulled my parents aside and said there was a restricted service road that would get us out quicker. My mom and dad were nervous—they wanted to stay with the main group, follow the rules. They said no. The guide insisted it was safe if we stayed close, that he knew the terrain, that he and another ranger could handle it. My parents still refused.

"Later, while people were distracted, my friend—who was on another truck—found me and said the guides were moving down that service road to help locate the lion and secure the area. 'Come on,' he said. 'We'll get a closer look at everything. We're with professionals. It'll be fine. Don't be a baby.'"

Johnny swallowed.

"I knew I wasn't supposed to go. But part of me wanted to prove I was man enough, not just the scared kid my parents treated me like. So we slipped off the truck and followed the guides at a distance.

"The bush got thicker. The guides motioned for us to stay back, but we kept inching closer. One guide whispered, 'There's a lion nearby. Do not move. Be absolutely silent.' My heart was pounding so hard I could hear it in my ears.

"My friend crept forward anyway—he wanted to *see* it. Crack! He stepped on a stick.

"A massive lion exploded out of the tall grass, grabbed my friend, and dragged him off before I could blink. 'Run!' the guide shouted. He bolted toward the main road. I couldn't move. How could I leave my friend? I took a few steps after the lion, and it whipped its head around, growling at me. I could already see my friend was gone."

He looked away, eyes wet, voice raw.

"After that, they closed half the park. Rangers swept the area. And I made a vow: I would never, ever break from the protection of my leaders again. I would listen to commanders, teachers, parents. I would follow the rules. That vow got wired in deep. So now... I *can't* go. I can't bring you and violate the vow I made to myself. I can't watch someone else die because I thought I knew better."

I could tell his story was helping him process more than just the mission. His downcast eyes revealed that he wanted to help me, but was confined to rules made from fear.

"Johnny, I understand," I said gently. "I've made vows to myself as well. But when a vow is made under duress—through shock and terror—it's meant to be revisited. You're not that boy anymore. And this isn't sneaking off for a thrill; it's walking toward a possibility of peace."

He met my eyes cautiously.

"We have a great opportunity," I continued, "but it will require one of two things: either I sneak off in the middle of the night without you, or you willingly come. If you're willing, let go of the vow you made as a grieving, scared boy and allow the love of God to heal that moment. Would you be willing to do that—for yourself?"

"How?" he asked. "Even if I wanted to, I don't know where to begin."

"Take a knee," I said softly. "And ask the following:

'Heavenly Creator, I know I broke rules and there were consequences. I then created new rules as a scared young boy. I release this fear and allow You to teach me what these rules mean for today.'"

He repeated the prayer, and his gaze shifted skyward.

I continued, "Now add this:

'I release trying to control the outcome of my friend's passing. I release trying to save my friend. I cancel the stories I told about how I might have changed the outcome. I invite love to come to me and heal my wounds everywhere.'"

With that, the tears came. He broke open, healing in real time.

He cried out, "God, why did you let the lion take him? Why

did my friend die? Why did You let that happen? You wrecked my whole life. I don't know how to trust You."

Despite his raging, I saw the progress he was making and prompted him with another prayer:

"God, show me who You actually are. I release trying to keep You in the box I've kept You in—as the persecutor of my life."

He repeated it, and another wave of energy moved through him. His breath deepened, releasing trauma, hurt, and pain.

I reminded Johnny to think of his friend before the attack—to remember the life that was in him. He paused and closed his eyes, seeing his friend's grin, their shared jokes, the spark in his eyes. Tapping into a vein of joy, Johnny smiled—his whole demeanor shifting.

"There," I said. "Now, ask God what the right action is. Upon asking, just wait. An answer will arise."

Johnny, now more comfortable with the process, did as I asked, and his face lit up.

"I think I got an answer," he said. "I see tents and the word 'GO' emblazoned above them. I'm in. I'll go with you."

We high-fived and felt a shared relief.

Soon we were on our way, packing up in the morning and heading to the riverbed. We followed the water for five miles before arriving at the tents. Three hundred yards in front of us, we stopped to inspect the scene. A dozen soldiers milled about the camp, with just a few standing guard.

Because they were expecting us, according to Timberwolf, I walked with courage toward the guards. They stopped us thirty yards away, ordering us to stay where we were. They approached, searched me, and took Johnny's weapons. They ushered me quickly into the middle tent.

What I saw inside horrified me: a man whose lower body had been crushed almost beyond recognition. Everything from his waist down was mangled, wrapped in blood-soaked bandages; one leg ended where the knee should have been, the other twisted and broken beneath layers of cloth. His torso rose from the stretcher like what was left of a tree trunk after a storm. That he was still breathing was a miracle.

He lay there, a woman sitting by his side. She asked if I could help him. I didn't know, for I had never seen such a wound.

"I'll consult with God," I said. "Leave me with him."

Despite mild hesitation, she left the tent.

I asked God what I could possibly do in this circumstance.

"Nothing," came the answer.

"Then why am I here, Lord? Why have You brought me here?"

"You will see. You will see."

I sat on a circular rug near the man, praying for about thirty minutes before my hands started moving involuntarily. One hand rested on the bandaged mess covering the man's head. The other hand covered his abdomen. I asked the holy love of God to pour through me and do whatever was necessary.

Within a few minutes, the nearly dead man gasped, and I saw something move through his body. It looked like tiny living sparks racing under his skin. My hands remained as these critters traversed to and fro, putting things back, replacing, creating, healing. Hallucination? Reality? I didn't know—but it was astonishing.

The energy surge in my body was different—the power of a jet engine compared to the propeller-level energy I'd been accustomed to. I felt my body grow lighter and lift from the ground. Though my eyes were closed, my inner sight showed angels and spiritual helpers arriving. They performed what looked like surgeries.

One angel turned to me and said, "You are a man who heals. That's why you see this. Your work will accelerate. We will teach many people how healing works. Witnessing this will align you more fully with God's presence. Call on God's holy angels to join you and whomever God chooses for you to work with. Now grab that cinch over there and let's pull him up. He's been crushed, and his spine needs to be elevated."

I followed the instructions and soon had his neck lifted by a scarf-like cloth. Standing behind him, I pulled back on one side and then the other, rocking his head to extend it away from his body. Almost cartoon-like, waves of energy morphed his body and stretched his spine. Bones lengthened, muscles returned, and his skin softened and healed. It was the rebirth of a human, but in fast-forward and outside the womb. Incredible.

Some might think this is an exaggeration, but the truth is no words could describe what actually happened. Can words describe a gourmet meal to someone who has only ever eaten fast food? No. Can words describe mountain skiing to someone who has only been sledding in their backyard? No. Can words describe the mystery of God's healing to our world of medicine? No. There's just no reference for God's glory.

Perhaps if you've seen the glory of God in the eyes of a newborn child, that might come close to what I experienced here. In those eyes, we see the glory of God and remember the beauty and essence of life that we have. We are experiencing this amazing God active in the world, and it's so unbelievable that we get to be here and have this remarkable experience. At that moment in the tent, what I participated in and witnessed was inexplicable.

Then it stopped. The lights from the angelic forces dimmed, my feet planted back on the floor, his head rested, and he spoke in a raspy voice.

"Thank you. You decided to come. Thank you."

I called the others and said, "Come, come see him, it's time." Then I left the tent.

One of the soldiers offered me a plate of food and a seat by the fire. She asked, "What happened in there?"

"I don't know," I answered honestly. "I've never seen anything like it."

I could tell she wanted to say more. She waited a moment and then shared, "He's a special man. God gave him to us as a gift. He's like you."

I looked up, unaware of what she meant. "Like me?"

"Yes, he heals people. He told us that if he were ever injured, Timberwolf was to find you. That you were the one."

"I'm the one?"

"That's what he said."

The soldier left me to eat and suggested I stick around. I wanted to stay now. I hadn't met someone like me before, and my curiosity—and calling—burned brighter than ever.

CHAPTER 10
THE FRAGRANCE OF GOD AMONG US

Johnny and I stayed in the enemy camp for several days, praying, helping where we could. The habits of hatred we'd been trained into softened quickly; the men and women around us were not monsters but mirrors — frightened, weary, hungry for hope. We even behaved at times as friends with our *enemies*.

They heralded us as heroes, repeating that we'd saved their kingdom. Being treated as honored guests softened Johnny's skepticism; initially, concluding we were prey sitting amongst lions in their den. Neither of us slept well that first night but made up for it the next.

We were only enemies because we were told to be. This frontier region of the Eastern Kingdoms had become the battleground for the world's superpowers — ancient villages caught in the crosswinds of a modern war. The old kingdoms kept their ancient names, though the world around them had long moved into drones, missiles, and mechanized armies. The superpowers scarred half the globe, and this stretch of the Eastern Kingdoms was one of many places where humanity was tearing itself apart.

Despite my curiosity, I was kept away from the injured man as medical supplies and traditional support arrived in the days following the healing. I was in the dark about his health progress, but encouraged to pray and remain onsite until he recovered fully.

One afternoon, Johnny and I sat at the fire pit chatting and drinking delicious coffee when a tall figure approached. It was a man wearing orange shorts, leather sandals, and a faded white and blue Hawaiian button-down. His long hair looked much like Timberwolf's, pulled back in a ponytail.

"Hello, friend," he said with delightful ease and calm. "What's that smell?" he asked.

"I don't know what you mean." I said. "Coffee perhaps?"

"No, there's a beautiful aroma I caught a whiff of as I approached you. What is it?"

"I don't know," I repeated. "Perhaps it's just us, the way we smell."

However, it wasn't a bodily fragrance, but something spiritual, the scent of a soul aligned. Some call it the fragrance of prayer.

"Well, you certainly have a beautiful fragrance emanating from your beings. Thank you again, Thomas. You are the one I knew you to be."

"What does that mean, 'the one'?" I asked. "And who are you?"

The man sat with us and shared, "I was shown an image of you four months ago, Thomas, and was told I'd meet you; that together, we would create a community of holy men and women, changing the trajectory of this war. We can offer a path to restored wholeness that radiates God's life force. Anyone who comes into contact with that field will receive divine guidance and be invited to contribute to God's holy plan. Individual and collective talents and gifts will emerge from the group, some previously blocked by sin and distortions in their lives. I imagine God's voice amplifying to be heard by many seeking that relationship. It will be like a radiant sun restored to a sunless universe, like rain in the desert.

"I had heard about you, Thomas, and desired to meet you, but didn't know where to look. Even if I located you, communications, as you know, have been hampered since the war. But I let Timberwolf know that if I were ever injured, he should go to a particular chapel and wait. If you were who I thought you were, you'd arrive. Well, you are aware of the rest, for you were prompted to find Timberwolf and chose to come here. I'm happy you did."

It was quite a story. Strange. Remarkable. Perfect. "So now what do we do?" I asked.

"We pray together. But first, let's prepare."

"Okay. By the way, what do I call you?" I asked.

"My name is Salome, but I wish you to call me friend."

I knew aligning myself this openly with an enemy leader might mark me a traitor in the eyes of my own, but the pull of God's presence was stronger than the fear of consequences.

Following his lead, we gathered firewood and discussed a plan. Upon returning to camp, Salome enlisted the soldiers to help build a temple. Within a few days, our makeshift temple, fashioned from tent materials, was ready. It had an air of sacred simplicity; its entrance marked by a flap of fabric adorned with symbols and colors conveying reverence. Inside, the ground was covered with a tarp, providing a humble yet comfortable area for worshipers to sit.

A small altar stood at the far end, constructed from stacked stones and draped with purple cloth. The altar held only two candles, a chalice, and a Bible that one of the women carried with her through every deployment — unopened for years and ready for its hour. I wondered if she had carried it all these years not knowing why — waiting, perhaps, for a moment such as this.

The sides of the temple were rolled up in sections to allow ventilation, light and views of the natural beauty surrounding the space. Despite its temporary nature, the temple exuded purpose and sanctity.

As we prayed, the community grew, and soon dozens of regulars made their way to the river for worship. It wasn't long before Salome's commanders came to investigate what had happened to him. Some heard he'd died in the battle. Upon hearing what actually happened, these commanders were incredulous, doubting our story was even moderately close to the truth. Yet, they allowed Johnny and me continued refuge in the camp, provided we continued to work with *Shalom*. That's what they called Salome, for he brought peace with him.

As the encampment grew, it buzzed with laughter and joy. I couldn't help but realize these people were just like our people, though happier at the moment. Why were we even fighting? Did anyone know?

I thought of Pablo then — how lost he had been, how violent his confusion. I prayed he would find the same mercy we were witnessing here. Word reached me weeks later: Pablo had laid down his weapons and asked for a blessing. Even the hardest stories were being rewritten.

We prayed constantly, and volunteers brought us water and meals throughout our prayers. But there were times when many hours passed with nothing to eat, just the presence of God in our midst.

Unlike the regime I'd come from — rigid, suspicious, and obsessed with control — these so-called enemies were spiritually starved and strangely open. They were ready. My old camp was not.

We taught all visitors the ways of health, right living, and clearing out all that was unlike God. The main lesson was to allow the Divine self to move out in front and for the human parts of sinfulness. To be forgiven and fall away like a tree trimmed of it's dead branches. All who were willing were stripped to the essence, their core where purity and love reigned. And in that space was God. They found God. They had been raised in a kingdom that feared God without knowing God. The seed of awe lived within them, now nourished to thrive.

As the weeks passed, the commanders grew to trust me and Johnny, who also participated fully in this process. One day, I was tapped on the shoulder by a commander who asked for help.

"I have a son and a daughter at home, and they're sick. Would you pray for them?" he asked. I said, of course. "No, you don't understand. They're dying. If I see them alive again, it would be incredible. My wife sent word that they may only have hours left. Please can we pray for them?"

I took him into the temple and asked Salome to join me with my new friend. The commander sat in a circle with us. I asked how he felt about his life. He didn't understand why I was asking about him, but obliged. He had killed many people and had tried to protect his side of the war, but he had no intention of living. He had every intention of dying a hero's death. He fairly certainly told his children they would need to take care of their home's needs if he were to die.

With guidance, he released his desire to die a hero's death. He was initially uncomfortable doing so, for he wanted people to remember him. That was his goal. He let that goal go along with his desire to die. I then said, "Now Salome and I can help your son and daughter heal."

"Why is that possible now and not before?" the man asked.

"Because you held on to this idea of dying, and your children fear caring for a home without you. You carried with you the angel of death, and they saw it. Salome and I saw it. This angel of death was with you to help you wake up and choose life. It is why you came to us. Now that you have chosen life, we can speak to the souls of your children and assure them that you will most certainly do everything you can to live. It's no guarantee, but at least they won't have a father carrying a death wish to the battlefield."

"Oh my gosh, you're right," he said. "I have been doing exactly that. I've been walking dead amongst the living, even when I was home. Of course, they picked up on it. Of course. Thank you, thank you, thank you."

Salome and I went to work, and the Commander departed for home. We imagined those children and spoke to their souls. Children feel what parents carry. His death-wish had suffocated their hope; releasing it gave their souls room to breathe.

Within a week, word reached us that the children were recovering. They would live. And in that moment, I felt something widening in the world — as though one man's surrender to life had unlatched a door for countless others to walk through.

As stories spread of the work Salome and I had been doing, a message arrived from the enemy's camp—well, not the enemy, but my old camp, for who was my enemy? They asked for my return (and Johnny). They perceived us being there as a hostile action and threatened severe repercussions. They wanted to exchange me for several prisoners. And requested that Salome and I serve both sides of the war. They wanted Salome, for they had heard the wonders associated with him.

And it happened this way for several months. Salome and I would go from one *enemy's* camp to another—or as we called it, one friend's camp to another. The people on each side joined together in larger and larger groups. No longer were we only working with the sick, but also the healthy. Awareness of God's love expanded. Those we helped, shared what they witnessed with others, and crowds grew.

Though always feeling responsible, our newfound notoriety gave us a voice beyond our ranks. Using this voice, Salome and I met with leadership on both sides, delivering a divinely gifted message: "It is time to end the war. You have been told in your dreams, and some of you while awake, that it's time. We are bringing it to the surface, reinforcing what you know in your hearts."

We could tell by the way their eyes shifted, and they squirmed uncomfortably that it was true. We pressed on. "Who among you has received such a message in whatever capacity?"

In the circles of leadership, many hands went up. They knew it was time.

"But what will we do with no war? What's next for all these people?" Both sides inquired.

"You will be made anew," I said, and Salome echoed, "Yes, you will be guided to new opportunities for your populations. You will thrive in ways you can't think about while you focus on war. You'll find joy in new adventures. The torment of war will fall from your minds. You will reconnect to your Source connection, heal your soul and live happier lives. What happens when you die in war?" Salome asked. "You go home, and that's what you'll open for all people under your command. You'll open the gates to restore the heavens to their earthly lives. You have that power. Just end the war."

The message was received, but the actions were slow. War continued for several months with less aggressiveness and diminishing will. Fewer people wanted to fight as more and more found their heaven as they healed in the spirit.

The war ended not with treaties or triumphs, but with exhaustion — a collective exhale as if humanity remembered, all at once, that it was tired of killing itself. Peace returned. The smells of summer carried on.

EPILOGUE
AND, SO WHAT

A deeper awareness of God is available to you—yes, you —just as it was for the characters in this story. Though they are fictional, their experiences draw from countless real encounters. This same relationship with God is available right now: hearing God's voice, tasting Heaven, receiving healing, and awakening extraordinary gifts.

Happiness, fulfillment, and joy rise naturally as we meet God in God's true nature—love.

Some may question this. Some may feel abandoned or unworthy. Having walked with hundreds of people through spiritual integration, I assure you:

You have not been abandoned.

You are not unworthy.

Jesus bridges the distance between how we see ourselves and how God sees us. And in every case, the stories that keep us from God fall apart, and truth restores itself. As that truth restores you, your perception of God will purify, and love will reveal itself again and again.

Continue the Journey

If you want to go deeper, The O Coalition offers many resources. Explore at thelowlyprophet.com/supportmission

• **Books** and practices rooted in Jesus' teachings

• **Community** committed to living as whole, Christ-centered beings

• **Free podcast** and live events — search *@theocoalition* on YouTube.

Please consider sharing this book with family, friends, and church leaders.

And please review it on Amazon — your review helps other seekers find these teachings.

Gratitude

Thank you. These books were given by God, and they are meant to open people to deeper wholeness in relationship with our Creator. Your willingness to read and receive is a blessing. I pray that, through this story, you have felt God's presence more fully.

Lastly

Heaven is here—closer than your breath.

You may or may not share Thomas's gifts, but you do carry gifts of your own. Just as the seed of an apple tree holds the promise of apples, you hold the seeds God placed in your spirit. If they are dormant, the tools in these books can nourish them into fruit.

Say yes to the true you.

Only resistance in your will can keep you from God's holy love.

God is saying "yes" to you even now.

Will you say "yes" to yourself?

Now, let us begin.

ACKNOWLEDGMENTS

To **God**, for this amazing story and all the stories I am blessed to receive and share. I am so thankful.

To Jesus and His eternal love for us.

To Melissa G. Wilson, for being the first to read and share input in this book's roughest state!

To people who support The O Coalition. Thanks for helping these stories reach the masses.

To Joseph Gabriel, who continues helping The O Coalition deliver high value!

To Illuminix Entertainment for helping our message get out via The O Coalition podcast (@theocoalition on YouTube).

To my **rockstart pre-release readers**, including James Chitwood, Phil Dugas, Joseph Gabriel, Alison Ooms, Gina Johnson, Stefan Junaeus, Dawn Kristy, Amy Lau, Kathy McGrath, Rex Montague Bauer, Robert Slayton, and Katie Wresch.

To **Milabookcovers.com** for the continued support on cover design.

To **Thought Leaders Press** and **Stefan Junaeus** for support in continuing to make this series a success. To **Leanne Huffman** for an amazing developmental and final edit. To **Chrysta Marquez** and **Lindsay Elston** for all the work in the final publishing details. Thanks for your commitment to excellence.

ABOUT THE AUTHOR

Mark Hattas is a successful entrepreneur and author. He is passionate about introducing people to the powerful practices Jesus shared for happiness and fulfillment. He went through a massive transformation following the sale of his tech business in 2010. Today, God's asked Mark to write. He writes fiction novels that deepen faith with people hungry to know how to live their optimal lives.

His attitude about writing: Give it to God and allow the story to come. And this is how every book in the series has excelled to deliver on a promise to support everyone who reads to find Christ in an intimate way—healing wounds of the past and arriving at a new life in union with God.

This is something he wishes everyone could know and experience. It has helped him have a new awareness of God, and invites us all to embrace this too.

The O Coalition collection began with book one, The Lowly

Prophet, which won six awards and opened the door for book two, The Veil Breaker. Enjoy the whole series and discover more at theocoalition.com.